William Butler Yeats

The Unicorn from the Stars and other plays

Outlook

William Butler Yeats

The Unicorn from the Stars and other plays

1. Auflage | ISBN: 978-3-73261-867-5

Erscheinungsort: Paderborn, Deutschland

Erscheinungsjahr: 2018

Outlook Verlag GmbH, Paderborn.

William Butler Yeats

The Unicorn from the Stars and other plays

Outlook

THE UNICORN FROM

THE STARS

AND OTHER PLAYS

BY

WILLIAM B. YEATS

AND

LADY GREGORY

New York
THE MACMILLAN COMPANY
1908

All rights reserved

New edition. Set up and electrotyped. Published April, 1908.

Norwood Press
J. S. Cushing Co.—Berwick & Smith Co.
Norwood, Mass., U.S.A.

1

PREFACE

About seven years ago I began to dictate the first of these Plays to Lady Gregory. My eyesight had become so bad that I feared I could henceforth write nothing with my own hands but verses, which, as Theophile Gautier has said, can be written with a burnt match. Our Irish Dramatic movement was just passing out of the hands of English Actors, hired because we knew of no Irish ones, and our little troop of Irish amateurs—as they were at the time— could not have too many Plays, for they would come to nothing without continued playing. Besides, it was exciting to discover, after the unpopularity of blank verse, what one could do with three Plays written in prose and founded on three public interests deliberately chosen,—religion, humour, patriotism. I planned in those days to establish a dramatic movement upon the popular passions, as the ritual of religion is established in the emotions that surround birth and death and marriage, and it was only the coming of the unclassifiable, uncontrollable, capricious, uncompromising genius of J. M. Synge that altered the direction of the movement and made it individual, critical, and combative. If his had not, some other stone would have blocked up the old way, for the public mind of Ireland, stupefied by prolonged intolerant organisation, can take but brief pleasure in the caprice that is in all art, whatever its subject, and, more commonly, can but hate unaccustomed personal reverie.

I had dreamed the subject of "Cathleen ni Houlihan," but found when I looked for words that I could not create peasant dialogue that would go nearer to peasant life than the dialogue in "The Land of Heart's Desire" or "The Countess Cathleen." Every artistic form has its own ancestry, and the more elaborate it is, the more is the writer constrained to symbolise rather than to represent life, until perhaps his ladies of fashion are shepherds and shepherdesses, as when Colin Clout came home again. I could not get away, no matter how closely I watched the country life, from images and dreams which had all too royal blood, for they were descended like the thought of every poet from all the conquering dreams of Europe, and I wished to make that high life mix into some rough contemporary life without ceasing to be itself, as so many old books and Plays have mixed it and so few modern, and to do this I added another knowledge to my own. Lady Gregory had written no Plays, but had, I discovered, a greater knowledge of the country mind and country speech than anybody I had ever met with, and nothing but a burden of knowledge could keep "Cathleen ni Houlihan" from the clouds. I needed less help for the "Hour-Glass," for the speech there is far from reality, and so the Play is almost wholly mine. When, however, I brought to her the general scheme for the "Pot of Broth," a little farce which seems rather imitative to-day, though it plays well enough, and of the first version of "The Unicorn," "Where there is Nothing," a five-act Play written in a fortnight to save it from a plagiarist, and tried to dictate them, her share grew more and more considerable. She would not allow me to put her name to these Plays, though I have always tried to explain her share in them, but has signed "The Unicorn from the Stars," which but for a good deal of the general plan and a single character and bits of another is wholly hers. I feel indeed that my best share in it is that idea, which I have been capable of expressing completely in criticism alone, of bringing together the rough life of the road and the frenzy that the poets have found in their ancient cellar,—a prophecy, as it were, of the time when it will be once again possible for a Dickens and a Shelley to be born in the one body.

The chief person of the earlier Play was very dominating, and I have grown to look upon this as a fault, though it increases the dramatic effect in a superficial way. We cannot sympathise with the man who sets his anger at once lightly and confidently to overthrow the order of the world, for such a man will seem to us alike insane and arrogant. But our hearts can go with him, as I think, if he speak with some humility, so far as his daily self carry him, out of a cloudy light of vision; for whether he understand or not, it may be that voices of angels and archangels have spoken in the cloud, and whatever wildness come upon his life, feet of theirs may well have trod the clusters. But a man so plunged in trance is of necessity somewhat still and silent, though it be perhaps the silence and the stillness of a lamp; and the movement of the Play as a whole, if we are to have time to hear him, must be without hurry or violence.

NOTES

I cannot give the full cast of "Cathleen ni Houlihan," which was first played at St. Teresa's Hall, Dublin, on April 3, 1902, for I have been searching the cupboard of the Abbey Theatre, where we keep old Play-bills, and can find no record of it, nor did the newspapers of the time mention more than the principals. Mr. W. G. Fay played the old countryman, and Miss Quinn his wife, while Miss Maude Gonne was Cathleen ni Houlihan, and very magnificently she played. The Play has been constantly revived, and has, I imagine, been played more often than any other, except perhaps Lady Gregory's "Spreading the News," at the Abbey Theatre, Dublin.

The "Hour-Glass" was first played at the Molesworth Hall, Dublin, on March 14, 1903, with the following cast:—

The Wise Man,	J. W. Digges
Bridget, his wife,	Maire T. Quinn
Her children,	Eithne and Padragan ni Shiubhlaigh
Her pupils,	{ P. I. Kelly,
	{ Seumas O'Sullivan
	{ P. Colum
	{ P. MacShiubhlaigh
The Angel,	Maire ni Shiubhlaigh
The Fool,	F. J. Fay

The Play has been revived many times since then as a part of the repertoire at the Abbey Theatre, Dublin.

"The Unicorn from the Stars" was first played at the Abbey Theatre on November 23, 1907, with the following cast:—

Father John	Ernest Vaughan
Thomas Hearne	Arthur Sinclair
Andrew Hearne	J. A. O'Rourke
Martin Hearne	F. J. Fay
Johnny Bacach	W. G. Fay
Paudeen	J. M. Kerrigan
Biddy Lally	Maire O'Neill
Nanny	Bridget O'Dempsey

CONTENTS

4

THE UNICORN FROM THE STARS

CHARACTERS

FATHER JOHN
THOMAS HEARNE *a coach builder.*
ANDREW HEARNE *his brother.*
MARTIN HEARNE *his nephew.*
JOHNNY BACACH }
PAUDEEN   } *beggars.*
BIDDY LALLY   }
NANNY   }

ACT I

SCENE: *Interior of a coach builder's workshop. Parts of a gilded coach, among them an ornament representing the lion and the unicorn.* THOMAS *working at a wheel.* FATHER JOHN *coming from door of inner room.*

FATHER JOHN. I have prayed over Martin. I have prayed a long time, but there is no move in him yet.

THOMAS. You are giving yourself too much trouble, Father. It's as good for you to leave him alone till the doctor's bottle will come. If there is any cure at all for what is on him, it is likely the doctor will have it.

FATHER JOHN. I think it is not doctor's medicine will help him in this case.

THOMAS. It will, it will. The doctor has his business learned well. If Andrew had gone to him the time I bade him, and had not turned again to bring yourself to the house, it is likely Martin would be walking at this time. I am loth to trouble you, Father, when the business is not of your own sort. Any doctor at all should be able, and well able, to cure the falling sickness.

FATHER JOHN. It is not any common sickness that is on him now.

THOMAS. I thought at the first it was gone asleep he was. But when shaking him and roaring at him failed to rouse him, I knew well it was the falling

7

sickness. Believe me, the doctor will reach it with his drugs.

FATHER JOHN. Nothing but prayer can reach a soul that is so far beyond the world as his soul is at this moment.

THOMAS. You are not saying that the life is gone out of him!

FATHER JOHN. No, no, his life is in no danger. But where he himself, the spirit, the soul, is gone, I cannot say. It has gone beyond our imaginings. He is fallen into a trance.

THOMAS. He used to be queer as a child, going asleep in the fields and coming back with talk of white horses he saw, and bright people like angels or whatever they were. But I mended that. I taught him to recognise stones beyond angels with a few strokes of a rod. I would never give in to visions or to trances.

FATHER JOHN. We who hold the faith have no right to speak against trance or vision. St. Teresa had them, St. Benedict, St. Anthony, St. Columcille. St. Catherine of Sienna often lay a long time as if dead.

THOMAS. That might be so in the olden time, but those things are gone out of the world now. Those that do their work fair and honest have no occasion to let the mind go rambling. What would send my nephew, Martin Hearne, into a trance, supposing trances to be in it, and he rubbing the gold on the lion and unicorn that he had taken in hand to make a good job of for the top of the coach?

FATHER JOHN [taking it up]. It is likely it was that sent him off. The flashing of light upon it would be enough to throw one that had a disposition to it into a trance. There was a very saintly man, though he was not of our church, he wrote a great book called "Mysterium Magnum," was seven days in a trance. Truth, or whatever truth he found, fell upon him like a bursting shower, and he a poor tradesman at his work. It was a ray of sunlight on a pewter vessel that was the beginning of all. [Goes to the door of inner room.] There is no stir in him yet. It is either the best thing or the worst thing can happen to anyone that is happening to him now.

THOMAS. And what in the living world can happen to a man that is asleep on his bed?

FATHER JOHN. There are some would answer you that it is to those who are awake that nothing happens, and it is they that know nothing. He is gone where all have gone for supreme truth.

8

THOMAS [*sitting down again and taking up tools*]. Well, maybe so. But work must go on and coach building must go on, and they will not go on the time there is too much attention given to dreams. A dream is a sort of a shadow, no profit in it to anyone at all. A coach now is a real thing and a thing that will last for generations and be made use of the last, and maybe turn to be a hen-roost at its latter end.

FATHER JOHN. I think Andrew told me it was a dream of Martin's that led to the making of that coach.

THOMAS. Well, I believe he saw gold in some dream, and it led him to want to make some golden thing, and coaches being the handiest, nothing would do him till he put the most of his fortune into the making of this golden coach. It turned out better than I thought, for some of the lawyers came looking at it at assize time, and through them it was heard of at Dublin Castle ... and who now has it ordered but the Lord Lieutenant! [FATHER JOHN *nods.*] Ready it must be and sent off it must be by the end of the month. It is likely King George will be visiting Dublin, and it is he himself will be sitting in it yet.

FATHER JOHN. Martin has been working hard at it, I know.

THOMAS. You never saw a man work the way he did, day and night, near ever since the time, six months ago, he first came home from France.

FATHER JOHN. I never thought he would be so good at a trade. I thought his mind was only set on books.

THOMAS. He should be thankful to myself for that. Any person I will take in hand I make a clean job of them the same as I would make of any other thing in my yard, coach, half coach, hackney-coach, ass car, common car, post-chaise, calash, chariot on two wheels, on four wheels. Each one has the shape Thomas Hearne put on it, and it in his hands; and what I can do with wood and iron, why would I not be able to do it with flesh and blood, and it in a way my own?

FATHER JOHN. Indeed I know you did your best for Martin.

THOMAS. Every best. Checked him, taught him the trade, sent him to the monastery in France for to learn the language and to see the wide world; but who should know that if you did not know it, Father John, and I doing it according to your own advice?

FATHER JOHN. I thought his nature needed spiritual guidance and teaching, the best that could be found.

9

THOMAS. I thought myself it was best for him to be away for a while. There are too many wild lads about this place. He to have stopped here, he might have taken some fancies and got into some trouble, going against the Government, maybe, the same as Johnny Gibbons that is at this time an outlaw having a price upon his head.

FATHER JOHN. That is so. That imagination of his might have taken fire here at home. It was better putting him with the Brothers, to turn it to imaginings of heaven.

THOMAS. Well, I will soon have a good hardy tradesman made of him now that will live quiet and rear a family, and maybe be appointed coach builder to the royal family at the last.

FATHER JOHN [*at window*]. I see your brother Andrew coming back from the doctor; he is stopping to talk with a troop of beggars that are sitting by the side of the road.

THOMAS. There now is another that I have shaped. Andrew used to be a bit wild in his talk and in his ways, wanting to go rambling, not content to settle in the place where he was reared. But I kept a guard over him; I watched the time poverty gave him a nip, and then I settled him into the business. He never was so good a worker as Martin; he is too fond of wasting his time talking vanities. But he is middling handy, and he is always steady and civil to customers. I have no complaint worth while to be making this last twenty years against Andrew. [ANDREW *comes in.*]

ANDREW. Beggars there are outside going the road to the Kinvara fair. They were saying there is news that Johnny Gibbons is coming back from France on the quiet. The king's soldiers are watching the ports for him.

THOMAS. Let you keep now, Andrew, to the business you have in hand. Will the doctor be coming himself, or did he send a bottle that will cure Martin?

ANDREW. The doctor can't come, for he is down with lumbago in the back. He questioned me as to what ailed Martin, and he got a book to go looking for a cure, and he began telling me things out of it, but I said I could not be carrying things of that sort in my head. He gave me the book then, and he has marks put in it for the places where the cures are … wait now … [*Reads.*] "Compound medicines are usually taken inwardly, or outwardly applied. Inwardly taken they should be either liquid or solid; outwardly they should be fomentations or sponges wet in some decoctions."

THOMAS. He had a right to have written it out himself upon a paper. Where is the use of all that?

ANDREW. I think I moved the mark maybe ... here now is the part he was reading to me himself ... "the remedies for diseases belonging to the skins next the brain: headache, vertigo, cramp, convulsions, palsy, incubus, apoplexy, falling sickness."

THOMAS. It is what I bid you to tell him—that it was the falling sickness.

ANDREW [dropping book]. O my dear, look at all the marks gone out of it. Wait now, I partly remember what he said ... a blister he spoke of ... or to be smelling hartshorn ... or the sneezing powder ... or if all fails, to try letting the blood.

FATHER JOHN. All this has nothing to do with the real case. It is all waste of time.

ANDREW. That is what I was thinking myself, Father. Sure it was I was the first to call out to you when I saw you coming down from the hillside and to bring you in to see what could you do. I would have more trust in your means than in any doctor's learning. And in case you might fail to cure him, I have a cure myself I heard from my grandmother ... God rest her soul ... and she told me she never knew it to fail. A person to have the falling sickness, to cut the top of his nails and a small share of the hair of his head, and to put it down on the floor and to take a harry-pin and drive it down with that into the floor and to leave it there. "That is the cure will never fail," she said, "to rise up any person at all having the falling sickness."

FATHER JOHN [hands on ears]. I will go back to the hillside, I will go back to the hillside, but no, no, I must do what I can, I will go again, I will wrestle, I will strive my best to call him back with prayer. [Goes into room and shuts door.]

ANDREW. It is queer Father John is sometimes, and very queer. There are times when you would say that he believes in nothing at all.

THOMAS. If you wanted a priest, why did you not get our own parish priest that is a sensible man, and a man that you would know what his thoughts are? You know well the Bishop should have something against Father John to have left him through the years in that poor mountainy place, minding the few unfortunate people that were left out of the last famine. A man of his learning to be going in rags the way he is, there must be some good cause for that.

11

Andrew. I had all that in mind and I bringing him. But I thought he would have done more for Martin than what he is doing. To read a Mass over him I thought he would, and to be convulsed in the reading it, and some strange thing to have gone out with a great noise through the doorway.

Thomas. It would give no good name to the place such a thing to be happening in it. It is well enough for labouring men and for half-acre men. It would be no credit at all such a thing to be heard of in this house, that is for coach building the capital of the county.

Andrew. If it is from the devil this sickness comes, it would be best to put it out whatever way it would be put out. But there might no bad thing be on the lad at all. It is likely he was with wild companions abroad, and that knocking about might have shaken his health. I was that way myself one time....

Thomas. Father John said that it was some sort of a vision or a trance, but I would give no heed to what he would say. It is his trade to see more than other people would see, the same as I myself might be seeing a split in a leather car hood that no other person would find out at all.

Andrew. If it is the falling sickness is on him, I have no objection to that ... a plain, straight sickness that was cast as a punishment on the unbelieving Jews. It is a thing that might attack one of a family and one of another family and not to come upon their kindred at all. A person to have it, all you have to do is not to go between him and the wind or fire or water. But I am in dread trance is a thing might run through the house, the same as the cholera morbus.

Thomas. In my belief there is no such thing as a trance. Letting on people do be to make the world wonder the time they think well to rise up. To keep them to their work is best, and not to pay much attention to them at all.

Andrew. I would not like trances to be coming on myself. I leave it in my will if I die without cause, a holly stake to be run through my heart the way I will lie easy after burial, and not turn my face downwards in my coffin. I tell you I leave it on you in my will.

Thomas. Leave thinking of your own comforts, Andrew, and give your mind to the business. Did the smith put the irons yet on to the shafts of this coach?

Andrew. I'll go see did he.

Thomas. Do so, and see did he make a good job of it. Let the shafts be sound and solid if they *are* to be studded with gold.

ANDREW. They are, and the steps along with them … glass sides for the people to be looking in at the grandeur of the satin within … the lion and the unicorn crowning all … it was a great thought Martin had the time he thought of making this coach!

THOMAS. It is best for me go see the smith myself … and leave it to no other one. You can be attending to that ass car out in the yard wants a new tyre in the wheel … out in the rear of the yard it is. [*They go to door.*] To pay attention to every small thing, and to fill up every minute of time, shaping whatever you have to do, that is the way to build up a business. [*They go out.*]

FATHER JOHN [*bringing in* MARTIN]. They are gone out now … the air is fresher here in the workshop … you can sit here for a while. You are now fully awake; you have been in some sort of a trance or a sleep.

MARTIN. Who was it that pulled at me? Who brought me back?

FATHER JOHN. It is I, Father John, did it. I prayed a long time over you and brought you back.

MARTIN. You, Father John, to be so unkind! O leave me, leave me alone!

FATHER JOHN. You are in your dream still.

MARTIN. It was no dream, it was real … do you not smell the broken fruit … the grapes … the room is full of the smell.

FATHER JOHN. Tell me what you have seen where you have been.

MARTIN. There were horses … white horses rushing by, with white, shining riders … there was a horse without a rider, and someone caught me up and put me upon him, and we rode away, with the wind, like the wind….

FATHER JOHN. That is a common imagining. I know many poor persons have seen that.

MARTIN. We went on, on, on … we came to a sweet-smelling garden with a gate to it … and there were wheat-fields in full ear around … and there were vineyards like I saw in France, and the grapes in bunches … I thought it to be one of the town-lands of heaven. Then I saw the horses we were on had changed to unicorns, and they began trampling the grapes and breaking them … I tried to stop them, but I could not.

FATHER JOHN. That is strange, that is strange. What is it that brings to mind … I heard it in some place, *Monocoros di Astris*, the Unicorn from the Stars.

13

MARTIN. They tore down the wheat and trampled it on stones, and then they tore down what were left of the grapes and crushed and bruised and trampled them … I smelt the wine, it was flowing on every side … then everything grew vague … I cannot remember clearly … everything was silent … the trampling now stopped … we were all waiting for some command. Oh! was it given! I was trying to hear it … there was some one dragging, dragging me away from that … I am sure there was a command given … and there was a great burst of laughter. What was it? What was the command? Everything seemed to tremble around me.

FATHER JOHN. Did you awake then?

MARTIN. I do not think I did … it all changed … it was terrible, wonderful. I saw the unicorns trampling, trampling … but not in the wine troughs…. Oh, I forget! Why did you waken me?

FATHER JOHN. I did not touch you. Who knows what hands pulled you away? I prayed; that was all I did. I prayed very hard that you might awake. If I had not, you might have died. I wonder what it all meant. The unicorns … what did the French monk tell me … strength they meant … virginal strength, a rushing, lasting, tireless strength.

MARTIN. They were strong…. Oh, they made a great noise with their trampling!

FATHER JOHN. And the grapes … what did they mean?… It puts me in mind of the psalm … *Ex calix meus inebrians quam praeclarus est.* It was a strange vision, a very strange vision, a very strange vision.

MARTIN. How can I get back to that place?

FATHER JOHN. You must not go back, you must not think of doing that; that life of vision, of contemplation, is a terrible life, for it has far more of temptation in it than the common life. Perhaps it would have been best for you to stay under rules in the monastery.

MARTIN. I could not see anything so clearly there. It is back here in my own place the visions come, in the place where shining people used to laugh around me and I a little lad in a bib.

FATHER JOHN. You cannot know but it was from the Prince of this world the vision came. How can one ever know unless one follows the discipline of the church? Some spiritual director, some wise, learned man, that is what you want. I do not know enough. What am I but a poor banished priest with my learning forgotten, my books never handled, and spotted with the damp?

MARTIN. I will go out into the fields where you cannot come to me to awake me … I will see that townland again … I will hear that command. I cannot wait, I must know what happened, I must bring that command to mind again.

FATHER JOHN [*putting himself between* MARTIN *and the door*]. You must have patience as the saints had it. You are taking your own way. If there is a command from God for you, you must wait His good time to receive it.

MARTIN. Must I live here forty years, fifty years … to grow as old as my uncles, seeing nothing but common things, doing work … some foolish work?

FATHER JOHN. Here they are coming. It is time for me to go. I must think and I must pray. My mind is troubled about you. [*To* THOMAS *as he and* ANDREW *come in.*] Here he is; be very kind to him, for he has still the weakness of a little child.

    [*Goes out.*]

THOMAS. Are you well of the fit, lad?

MARTIN. It was no fit. I was away … for a while … no, you will not believe me if I tell you.

ANDREW. I would believe it, Martin. I used to have very long sleeps myself and very queer dreams.

THOMAS. You had, till I cured you, taking you in hand and binding you to the hours of the clock. The cure that will cure yourself, Martin, and will waken you, is to put the whole of your mind on to your golden coach, to take it in hand, and to finish it out of face.

MARTIN. Not just now. I want to think … to try and remember what I saw, something that I heard, that I was told to do.

THOMAS. No, but put it out of your mind. There is no man doing business that can keep two things in his head. A Sunday or a Holyday now you might go see a good hurling or a thing of the kind, but to be spreading out your mind on anything outside of the workshop on common days, all coach building would come to an end.

MARTIN. I don't think it is building I want to do. I don't think that is what was in the command.

THOMAS. It is too late to be saying that the time you have put the most of your fortune in the business. Set yourself now to finish your job, and when it is ended, maybe I won't begrudge you going with the coach as far as Dublin.

ANDREW. That is it; that will satisfy him. I had a great desire myself, and I young, to go travelling the roads as far as Dublin. The roads are the great things; they never come to an end. They are the same as the serpent having his tail swallowed in his own mouth.

MARTIN. It was not wandering I was called to. What was it? What was it?

THOMAS. What you are called to, and what everyone having no great estate is called to, is to work. Sure the world itself could not go on without work.

MARTIN. I wonder if that is the great thing, to make the world go on. No, I don't think that is the great thing ... what does the Munster poet call it ... "this crowded slippery coach-loving world." I don't think I was told to work for that.

ANDREW. I often thought that myself. It is a pity the stock of the Hearnes to be asked to do any work at all.

THOMAS. Rouse yourself, Martin, and don't be talking the way a fool talks. You started making that golden coach, and you were set upon it, and you had me tormented about it. You have yourself wore out working at it and planning it and thinking of it, and at the end of the race, when you have the winning post in sight, and horses hired for to bring it to Dublin Castle, you go falling into sleeps and blathering about dreams, and we run to a great danger of letting the profit and the sale go by. Sit down on the bench now, and lay your hands to the work.

MARTIN [*sitting down*]. I will try. I wonder why I ever wanted to make it; it was no good dream set me doing that. [*He takes up wheel.*] What is there in a wooden wheel to take pleasure in it? Gilding it outside makes it no different.

THOMAS. That is right now. You had some good plan for making the axle run smooth.

MARTIN [*letting wheel fall and putting his hands to his head*]. It is no use. [*Angrily.*] Why did you send the priest to awake me? My soul is my own and my mind is my own. I will send them to where I like. You have no authority over my thoughts.

THOMAS. That is no way to be speaking to me. I am head of this business. Nephew or no nephew, I will have no one come cold or unwilling to the work.

MARTIN. I had better go. I am of no use to you. I am going…. I must be alone…. I will forget if I am not alone. Give me what is left of my money, and I will go out of this.

THOMAS [*opening a press and taking out a bag and throwing it to him*]. There is what is left of your money! The rest of it you have spent on the coach. If you want to go, go, and I will not have to be annoyed with you from this out.

ANDREW. Come now with me, Thomas. The boy is foolish, but it will soon pass over. He has not my sense to be giving attention to what you will say. Come along now; leave him for a while; leave him to me, I say; it is I will get inside his mind.

[*He leads* THOMAS *out.* MARTIN, *when they have gone, sits down, taking up lion and unicorn.*]

MARTIN. I think it was some shining thing I saw…. What was it?

ANDREW [*opening door and putting in his head*]. Listen to me, Martin.

MARTIN. Go away—no more talking—leave me alone.

ANDREW [*coming in*]. Oh, but wait. I understand you. Thomas doesn't understand your thoughts, but I understand them. Wasn't I telling you I was just like you once?

MARTIN. Like me? Did you ever see the other things, the things beyond?

ANDREW. I did. It is not the four walls of the house keep me content. Thomas doesn't know, oh, no, he doesn't know.

MARTIN. No, he has no vision.

ANDREW. He has not, nor any sort of a heart for frolic.

MARTIN. He has never heard the laughter and the music beyond.

ANDREW. He has not, nor the music of my own little flute. I have it hidden in the thatch outside.

MARTIN. Does the body slip from you as it does from me? They have not shut your window into eternity?

ANDREW. Thomas never shut a window I could not get through. I knew you were one of my own sort. When I am sluggish in the morning Thomas says, "Poor Andrew is getting old." That is all he knows. The way to keep young is to do the things youngsters do. Twenty years I have been slipping away, and

17

he never found me out yet!

MARTIN. That is what they call ecstasy, but there is no word that can tell out very plain what it means. That freeing of the mind from its thoughts. Those wonders we know; when we put them into words, the words seem as little like them as blackberries are like the moon and sun.

ANDREW. I found that myself the time they knew me to be wild, and used to be asking me to say what pleasure did I find in cards, and women, and drink.

MARTIN. You might help me to remember that vision I had this morning, to understand it. The memory of it has slipped from me. Wait; it is coming back, little by little. I know that I saw the unicorns trampling, and then a figure, a many-changing figure, holding some bright thing. I knew something was going to happen or to be said, … something that would make my whole life strong and beautiful like the rushing of the unicorns, and then, and then….

JOHNNY BACACH'S VOICE [*at window*]. A poor person I am, without food, without a way, without portion, without costs, without a person or a stranger, without means, without hope, without health, without warmth….

ANDREW [*looking towards window*]. It is that troop of beggars; bringing their tricks and their thieveries they are to the Kinvara fair.

MARTIN [*impatiently*]. There is no quiet … come to the other room. I am trying to remember….

[*They go to door of inner room, but* ANDREW *stops him.*]

ANDREW. They are a bad-looking fleet. I have a mind to drive them away, giving them a charity.

MARTIN. Drive them away or come away from their voices.

ANOTHER VOICE. I put under the power of my prayer,

> All that will give me help,
>
> Rafael keep him Wednesday;
>
> Sachiel feed him Thursday;
>
> Hamiel provide him Friday;
>
> Cassiel increase him Saturday.

Sure giving to us is giving to the Lord and laying up a store in the treasury of heaven.

ANDREW. Whisht! He is coming in by the window! [JOHNNY B. *climbs in.*]

JOHNNY B. That I may never sin, but the place is empty!

PAUDEEN. Go in and see what can you make a grab at.

JOHNNY B. [*getting in*]. That every blessing I gave may be turned to a curse on them that left the place so bare! [*He turns things over.*] I might chance something in this chest if it was open…. [ANDREW *begins creeping towards him.*]

NANNY [*outside*]. Hurry on now, you limping crabfish, you! We can't be stopping here while you'll boil stirabout!

JOHNNY B. [*seizing bag of money and holding it up in both hands*]. Look at this now, look! [ANDREW *comes behind and seizes his arm.*]

JOHNNY B. [*letting bag fall with a crash*]. Destruction on us all!

MARTIN [*running forward, seizes him. Heads disappear*]. That is it! Oh, I remember! That is what happened! That is the command! Who was it sent you here with that command?

JOHNNY B. It was misery sent me in and starvation and the hard ways of the world.

NANNY [*outside*]. It was that, my poor child, and my one son only. Show mercy to him now, and he after leaving gaol this morning.

MARTIN [*to ANDREW.*]. I was trying to remember it … when he spoke that word it all came back to me. I saw a bright, many-changing figure … it was holding up a shining vessel … [*holds up arms*] then the vessel fell and was broken with a great crash … then I saw the unicorns trampling it. They were breaking the world to pieces … when I saw the cracks coming, I shouted for joy! And I heard the command, "Destroy, destroy; destruction is the life- giver; destroy."

ANDREW. What will we do with him? He was thinking to rob you of your gold.

MARTIN. How could I forget it or mistake it? It has all come upon me now … the reasons of it all, like a flood, like a flooded river.

JOHNNY B. [*weeping*]. It was the hunger brought me in and the drouth.

MARTIN. Were you given any other message? Did you see the unicorns?

JOHNNY B. I saw nothing and heard nothing; near dead I am with the fright I got and with the hardship of the gaol.

MARTIN. To destroy ... to overthrow all that comes between us and God, between us and that shining country. To break the wall, Andrew, the thing, whatever it is that comes between, but where to begin?...

ANDREW. What is it you are talking about?

MARTIN. It may be that this man is the beginning. He has been sent ... the poor, they have nothing, and so they can see heaven as we cannot. He and his comrades will understand me. But now to give all men high hearts that they may all understand.

JOHNNY B. It's the juice of the grey barley will do that.

ANDREW. To rise everybody's heart, is it? Is it that was your meaning?... If you will take the blame of it all, I'll do what you want. Give me the bag of money, then. [*He takes it up.*] Oh, I've a heart like your own! I'll lift the world too! The people will be running from all parts. Oh, it will be a great day in this district.

JOHNNY B. Will I go with you?

MARTIN. No, you must stay here; we have things to do and to plan.

JOHNNY B. Destroyed we all are with the hunger and the drouth.

MARTIN. Go then, get food and drink, whatever is wanted to give you strength and courage; gather your people together here; bring them all in. We have a great thing to do. I have to begin ... I want to tell it to the whole world. Bring them in, bring them in, I will make the house ready.

ACT II

SCENE: The same workshop a few minutes later. MARTIN. seen arranging mugs and bread, etc., on a table. FATHER JOHN comes in, knocking at open door as he comes.

MARTIN. Come in, come in, I have got the house ready. Here is bread and meat ... everybody is welcome. [Hearing no answer, turns round.]

FATHER JOHN. Martin, I have come back.... There is something I want to say to you.

MARTIN. You are welcome; there are others coming.... They are not of your sort, but all are welcome.

FATHER JOHN. I have remembered suddenly something that I read when I was in the seminary.

MARTIN. You seem very tired.

FATHER JOHN [*sitting down*]. I had almost got back to my own place when I thought of it. I have run part of the way. It is very important. It is about the trance that you have been in. When one is inspired from above, either in trance or in contemplation, one remembers afterwards all that one has seen and read. I think there must be something about it in St. Thomas. I know that I have read a long passage about it years ago. But, Martin, there is another kind of inspiration, or rather an obsession or possession. A diabolical power comes into one's body or overshadows it. Those whose bodies are taken hold of in this way, jugglers and witches and the like, can often tell what is happening in distant places, or what is going to happen, but when they come out of that state, they remember nothing. I think you said——

MARTIN. That I could not remember.

FATHER JOHN You remembered something, but not all. Nature is a great sleep; there are dangerous and evil spirits in her dreams, but God is above Nature. She is a darkness, but He makes everything clear—He is light.

MARTIN. All is clear now. I remember all, or all that matters to me. A poor man brought me a word, and I know what I have to do.

FATHER JOHN. Ah, I understand; words were put into his mouth. I have read of such things. God sometimes uses some common man as His messenger.

MARTIN. You may have passed the man who brought it on the road. He left me but now.

FATHER JOHN. Very likely, very likely, that is the way it happened. Some plain, unnoticed man has sometimes been sent with a command.

MARTIN. I saw the unicorns trampling in my dream. They were breaking the world. I am to destroy, that is the word the messenger spoke.

FATHER JOHN. To destroy?

MARTIN. To bring again the old disturbed exalted life, the old splendour. FATHER JOHN. You are not the first that dream has come to. [*Gets up and walks*

21

up and down.] It has been wandering here and there, calling now to this man, now to that other. It is a terrible dream.

MARTIN. Father John, you have had the same thought.

FATHER JOHN. Men were holy then; there were saints everywhere, there was reverence, but now it is all work, business, how to live a long time. Ah, if one could change it all in a minute, even by war and violence.... There is a cell where St. Ciaran used to pray, if one could bring that time again.

MARTIN. Do not deceive me. You have had the command.

FATHER JOHN. Why are you questioning me? You are asking me things that I have told to no one but my confessor.

MARTIN. We must gather the crowds together, you and I.

FATHER JOHN. I have dreamed your dream; it was long ago. I had your vision.

MARTIN. And what happened?

FATHER JOHN [*harshly*]. It was stopped. That was an end. I was sent to the lonely parish where I am, where there was no one I could lead astray. They have left me there. We must have patience; the world was destroyed by water, it has yet to be consumed by fire.

MARTIN. Why should we be patient? To live seventy years, and others to come after us and live seventy years it may be, and so from age to age, and all the while the old splendour dying more and more.

[A noise of shouting. ANDREW, who has been standing at the door for a moment, comes in.]

ANDREW. Martin says truth, and he says it well. Planing the side of a cart or a shaft, is that life? It is not. Sitting at a desk writing letters to the man that wants a coach or to the man that won't pay for the one he has got, is that life, I ask you? Thomas arguing at you and putting you down, "Andrew, dear Andrew, did you put the tyre on that wheel yet?" Is that life? No, it is not. I ask you all what do you remember when you are dead? It's the sweet cup in the corner of the widow's drinking house that you remember. Ha, ha, listen to that shouting! That is what the lads in the village will remember to the last day they live!

MARTIN. Why are they shouting? What have you told them?

ANDREW. Never you mind. You left that to me. You bade me to lift their hearts, and I did lift them. There is not one among them but will have his head like a blazing tar barrel before morning. What did your friend, the beggar, say? The juice of the grey barley, he said.

FATHER JOHN. You accursed villain! You have made them drunk!

ANDREW. Not at all, but lifting them to the stars. That is what Martin bade me to do, and there is no one can say I did not do it.

[*A shout at door and beggars push in a barrel. They all cry, "Hi! for the noble master!" and point at* ANDREW.]

JOHNNY B. It's not him, it's that one!

[*Points at* MARTIN.]

FATHER JOHN. Are you bringing this devil's work in at the very door? Go out of this, I say! Get out! Take these others with you!

MARTIN. No, no, I asked them in; they must not be turned out. They are my guests.

FATHER JOHN. Drive them out of your uncle's house!

MARTIN. Come, Father, it is better for you to go. Go back to your own place. I have taken the command. It is better, perhaps, for you that you did not take it. [MARTIN *and* FATHER JOHN *go out.*]

BIDDY. It is well for that old lad he didn't come between ourselves and our luck. It would be right to have flayed him and to have made bags of his skin.

NANNY. What a hurry you are in to get your enough! Look at the grease on your frock yet with the dint of the dabs you put in your pocket! Doing cures and foretellings, is it? You starved pot picker, you!

BIDDY. That you may be put up to-morrow to take the place of that decent son of yours that had the yard of the gaol wore with walking it till this morning!

NANNY. If he had, he had a mother to come to, and he would know her when he did see her, and that is what no son of your own could do, and he to meet you at the foot of the gallows!

JOHNNY B. If I did know you, I knew too much of you since the first beginning of my life! What reward did I ever get travelling with you? What store did you give me of cattle or of goods? What provision did I get from you by day or by night but your own bad character to be joined on to my own, and I following at your heels, and your bags tied round about me?

NANNY. Disgrace and torment on you! Whatever you got from me, it was more than any reward or any bit I ever got from the father you had, or any honourable thing at all, but only the hurt and the harm of the world and its shame!

JOHNNY B. What would he give you, and you going with him without leave? Crooked and foolish you were always, and you begging by the side of the ditch.

NANNY. Begging or sharing, the curse of my heart upon you! It's better off I was before ever I met with you, to my cost! What was on me at all that I did not cut a scourge in the wood to put manners and decency on you the time you were not hardened as you are!

JOHNNY B. Leave talking to me of your rods and your scourges! All you taught me was robbery, and it is on yourself and not on myself the scourges will be laid at the day of the recognition of tricks.

PAUDEEN. Faith, the pair of you together is better than Hector fighting before Troy!

NANNY. Ah, let you be quiet. It is not fighting we are craving, but the easing of the hunger that is on us and of the passion of sleep. Lend me a graineen of tobacco till I'll kindle my pipe—a blast of it will take the weight of the road off my heart.

[ANDREW *gives her some.* NANNY. *grabs at it.*]

BIDDY. No, but it's to myself you should give it. I that never smoked a pipe this forty year without saying the tobacco prayer. Let that one say, did ever she do that much?

NANNY. That the pain of your front tooth may be in your back tooth, you to be grabbing my share! [*They snap at tobacco.*]

ANDREW. Pup, pup, pup. Don't be snapping and quarrelling now, and you so well treated in this house. It is strollers like yourselves should be for frolic and for fun. Have you ne'er a good song to sing, a song that will rise all our hearts?

PAUDEEN. Johnny Bacach is a good singer; it is what he used to be doing in the fairs, if the oakum of the gaol did not give him a hoarseness in the throat.

ANDREW. Give it out so, a good song; a song will put courage and spirit into any man at all.

JOHNNY B. [*singing*].

Come, all ye airy bachelors,

A warning take by me:

A sergeant caught me fowling,

And fired his gun so free.

His comrades came to his relief,

And I was soon trepanned;

And, bound up like a woodcock,

Had fallen into their hands.

The judge said transportation;

The ship was on the strand;

They have yoked me to the traces

For to plough Van Dieman's land!

ANDREW. That's no good of a song, but a melancholy sort of a song. I'd as lief be listening to a saw going through timber. Wait, now, till you will hear myself giving out a tune on the flute. [*Goes out for it.*]

JOHNNY B. It is what I am thinking there must be a great dearth and a great scarcity of good comrades in this place, a man like that youngster having means in his hand to be bringing ourselves and our rags into the house.

PAUDEEN. You think yourself very wise, Johnny Bacach. Can you tell me now who that man is?

JOHNNY B. Some decent lad, I suppose, with a good way of living and a mind to send up his name upon the roads.

PAUDEEN. You that have been gaoled this eight months know little of this countryside…. It isn't a limping stroller like yourself the boys would let come among them. But I know. I went to the drill a few nights, and I skinning kids for the mountainy men. In a quarry beyond the drill is … they have their plans made…. It's the square house of the Browns is to be made an attack on and plundered. Do you know now who is the leader they are waiting for?

JOHNNY B. How would I know that?

PAUDEEN [*singing*].

Oh, Johnny Gibbons, my five hundred healths to you.

It is long you are away from us over the sea!

JOHNNY B. [*standing up excitedly*]. Sure that man could not be John Gibbons that is outlawed.

PAUDEEN. I asked news of him from the old lad [*points after* ANDREW], and I bringing in the drink along with him. "Don't be asking questions," says he; "take the treat he gives you," says he. "If a lad that had a high heart has a mind to rouse the neighbours," says he, "and to stretch out his hand to all that pass the road, it is in France he learned it," says he, "the place he is but lately come from, and where the wine does be standing open in tubs. Take your treat when you get it," says he, "and make no delay, or all might be discovered and put an end to."

JOHNNY B. He came over the sea from France! It is Johnny Gibbons surely, but it seems to me they were calling him by some other name.

PAUDEEN. A man on his keeping might go by a hundred names. Would he be telling it out to us that he never saw before, and we with that clutch of chattering women along with us? Here he is coming now. Wait till you see is he the lad I think him to be.

MARTIN [*coming in*]. I will make my banner; I will paint the Unicorn on it. Give me that bit of canvas; there is paint over here. We will get no help from the settled men—we will call to the lawbreakers, the tinkers—the sievemakers— the sheep-stealers. [*He begins to make banner.*]

BIDDY. That sounds to be a queer name of an army. Ribbons I can understand, Whiteboys, Rightboys, Threshers, and Peep-o'-day, but Unicorns I never heard of before.

JOHNNY B. It is not a queer name, but a very good name. [*Takes up Lion and Unicorn.*] It is often you saw that before you in the dock. There is the Unicorn with the one horn, and what is it he is going against? The Lion of course. When he has the Lion destroyed, the Crown must fall and be shivered. Can't you see? It is the League of the Unicorns is the league that will fight and destroy the power of England and King George.

PAUDEEN. It is with that banner we will march and the lads in the quarry with us; it is they will have the welcome before him! It won't be long till we'll be attacking the Square House! Arms there are in it; riches that would smother the world; rooms full of guineas—we will put wax on our shoes walking them; the horses themselves shod with no less than silver!

MARTIN [*holding up the banner*]. There it is ready! We are very few now, but the army of the Unicorns will be a great army! [*To* JOHNNY B.] Why have you brought me the message? Can you remember any more? Has anything more come to you? Who told you to come to me? Who gave you the message?... Can you see anything or hear anything that is beyond the world?

JOHNNY B. I cannot. I don't know what do you want me to tell you at all.

MARTIN. I want to begin the destruction, but I don't know where to begin ... you do not hear any other voice?

JOHNNY B. I do not. I have nothing at all to do with freemasons or witchcraft.

PAUDEEN. It is Biddy Lally has to do with witchcraft. It is often she threw the cups and gave out prophecies the same as Columcille.

MARTIN. You are one of the knowledgeable women. You can tell me where it is best to begin, and what will happen in the end.

BIDDY. I will foretell nothing at all. I rose out of it this good while, with the stiffness and the swelling it brought upon my joints.

MARTIN. If you have foreknowledge, you have no right to keep silent. If you do not help me, I may go to work in the wrong way. I know I have to destroy, but when I ask myself what I am to begin with, I am full of uncertainty.

PAUDEEN. Here now are the cups handy and the leavings in them.

BIDDY [*taking cups and pouring one from another*]. Throw a bit of white money into the four corners of the house.

MARTIN. There! [*Throwing it.*]

BIDDY. There can be nothing told without silver. It is not myself will have the profit of it. Along with that I will be forced to throw out gold.

MARTIN. There is a guinea for you. Tell me what comes before your eyes.

BIDDY. What is it you are wanting to have news of?

MARTIN. Of what I have to go out against at the beginning ... there is so much ... the whole world, it may be.

BIDDY [*throwing from one cup to another and looking*]. You have no care for yourself. You have been across the sea; you are not long back. You are coming within the best day of your life.

MARTIN. What is it? What is it I have to do?

BIDDY. I see a great smoke, I see burning … there is a great smoke overhead.

MARTIN. That means we have to burn away a great deal that men have piled up upon the earth. We must bring men once more to the wildness of the clean green earth.

BIDDY. Herbs for my healing, the big herb and the little herb; it is true enough they get their great strength out of the earth.

JOHNNY B. Who was it the green sod of Ireland belonged to in the olden times? Wasn't it to the ancient race it belonged? And who has possession of it now but the race that came robbing over the sea? The meaning of that is to destroy the big houses and the towns, and the fields to be given back to the ancient race.

MARTIN. That is it. You don't put it as I do, but what matter? Battle is all.

PAUDEEN. Columcille said the four corners to be burned, and then the middle of the field to be burned. I tell you it was Columcille's prophecy said that.

BIDDY. Iron handcuffs I see and a rope and a gallows, and it maybe is not for yourself I see it, but for some I have acquaintance with a good way back.

MARTIN. That means the law. We must destroy the law. That was the first sin, the first mouthful of the apple.

JOHNNY B. So it was, so it was. The law is the worst loss. The ancient law was for the benefit of all. It is the law of the English is the only sin.

MARTIN. When there were no laws men warred on one another and man to man, not with one machine against another as they do now, and they grew hard and strong in body. They were altogether alive like Him that made them in His image, like people in that unfallen country. But presently they thought it better to be safe, as if safety mattered, or anything but the exaltation of the heart and to have eyes that danger had made grave and piercing. We must overthrow the laws and banish them!

JOHNNY B. It is what I say, to put out the laws is to put out the whole nation of the English. Laws for themselves they made for their own profit and left us nothing at all, no more than a dog or a sow.

BIDDY. An old priest I see, and I would not say is he the one was here or another. Vexed and troubled he is, kneeling fretting, and ever fretting, in some lonesome, ruined place.

MARTIN. I thought it would come to that. Yes, the church too ... that is to be destroyed. Once men fought with their desires and their fears, with all that they call their sins, unhelped, and their souls became hard and strong. When we have brought back the clean earth and destroyed the law and the church, all life will become like a flame of fire, like a burning eye.... Oh, how to find words for it all ... all that is not life will pass away!

JOHNNY B. It is Luther's church he means, and the humpbacked discourse of Seaghan Calvin's Bible. So we will break it and make an end of it.

MARTIN [rising]. We will go out against the world and break it and unmake it. We are the army of the Unicorn from the Stars! We will trample it to pieces. We will consume the world, we will burn it away. Father John said the world has yet to be consumed by fire. Bring me fire.

ANDREW. Here is Thomas coming! [All except MARTIN hurry into next room. THOMAS comes in.]

THOMAS. Come with me, Martin. There is terrible work going on in the town! There is mischief gone abroad! Very strange things are happening!

MARTIN. What are you talking of? What has happened?

THOMAS. Come along, I say; it must be put a stop to! We must call to every decent man!... It is as if the devil himself had gone through the town on a blast and set every drinking house open!

MARTIN. I wonder how that has happened. Can it have anything to do with Andrew's plan?

THOMAS. Are you giving no heed to what I'm saying? There is not a man, I tell you, in the parish, and beyond the parish, but has left the work he was doing, whether in the field or in the mill.

MARTIN. Then all work has come to an end? Perhaps that was a good thought of Andrew's.

THOMAS. There is not a man has come to sensible years that is not drunk or drinking! My own labourers and my own serving-man are sitting on counters and on barrels! I give you my word the smell of the spirits and the porter and the shouting and the cheering within made the hair to rise up on my scalp.

MARTIN. And there is not one of them that does not feel that he could bridle the four winds.

THOMAS [sitting down in despair]. You are drunk, too. I never thought you had a fancy for it.

MARTIN. It is hard for you to understand. You have worked all your life. You have said to yourself every morning, "What is to be done to-day?" and when you are tired out you have thought of the next day's work. If you gave yourself an hour's idleness, it was but that you might work the better. Yet it is only when one has put work away that one begins to live.

THOMAS. It is those French wines that did it.

MARTIN. I have been beyond the earth, in paradise, in that happy townland. I have seen the shining people. They were all doing one thing or another, but not one of them was at work. All that they did was but the overflowing of their idleness, and their days were a dance bred of the secret frenzy of their hearts, or a battle where the sword made a sound that was like laughter.

THOMAS. You went away sober from out of my hands; they had a right to have minded you better.

MARTIN. No man can be alive, and what is paradise but fulness of life, if whatever he sets his hand to in the daylight cannot carry him from exaltation to exaltation, and if he does not rise into the frenzy of contemplation in the night silence. Events that are not begotten in joy are misbegotten and darken the world, and nothing is begotten in joy if the joy of a thousand years has not been crushed into a moment.

THOMAS. And I offered to let you go to Dublin in the coach! [ANDREW *and the beggars have returned cautiously.*]

MARTIN [*giving banner to* PAUDEEN]. Give me the lamp. The lamp has not yet been lighted, and the world is to be consumed! [*Goes into inner room.*]

THOMAS [*seeing* ANDREW]. Is it here you are, Andrew? What are the beggars doing? Was this door thrown open, too?... Why did you not keep order? I will go for the constables to help us!

ANDREW. You will not find them to help you. They were scattering themselves through the drinking houses of the town; and why wouldn't they?

THOMAS. Are you drunk, too? You are worse than Martin. You are a disgrace.

ANDREW. Disgrace yourself! Coming here to be making an attack on me and badgering me and disparaging me. And what about yourself that turned me to be a hypocrite?

THOMAS. What are you saying?

ANDREW. You did, I tell you. Weren't you always at me to be regular and to be working and to be going through the day and the night without company and to be thinking of nothing but the trade? What did I want with a trade? I got a sight of the fairy gold one time in the mountains. I would have found it again and brought riches from it but for you keeping me so close to the work.

THOMAS. Oh, of all the ungrateful creatures! You know well that I cherished you, leading you to live a decent, respectable life.

ANDREW. You never had respect for the ancient ways. It is after the mother you take it, that was too soft and too lumpish, having too much of the English in her blood. Martin is a Hearne like myself. It is he has the generous heart! It is not Martin would make a hypocrite of me and force me to do night walking secretly, watching to be back by the setting of the seven stars! [*He begins to play his flute.*]

THOMAS. I will turn you out of this, yourself and this filthy troop! I will have them lodged in gaol.

JOHNNY B. Filthy troop, is it? Mind yourself! The change is coming! The pikes will be up and the traders will go down!

[*All seize him and sing.*]

When the Lion shall lose his strength,

And the braket thistle begin to pine,—

The harp shall sound sweet, sweet at length

Between the eight and the nine!

THOMAS. Let me out of this, you villains!

NANNY. We'll make a sieve of holes of you, you old bag of treachery!

BIDDY. How well you threatened us with gaol! You skim of a weasel's milk!

JOHNNY B. You heap of sicknesses! You blinking hangman! That you may never die till you'll get a blue hag for a wife!

[MARTIN *comes back with lighted lamp.*]

MARTIN. Let him go. [*They let* THOMAS *go and fall back.*] Spread out the banner. The moment has come to begin the war.

JOHNNY B. Up with the Unicorn and destroy the Lion! Success to Johnny Gibbons and all good men!

MARTIN. Heap all those things together there. Heap those pieces of the coach one upon another. Put that straw under them. It is with this flame I will begin the work of destruction. All nature destroys and laughs.

THOMAS. Destroy your own golden coach!

MARTIN [*kneeling*]. I am sorry to go a way that you do not like, and to do a thing that will vex you. I have been a great trouble to you since I was a child in the house, and I am a great trouble to you yet. It is not my fault. I have been chosen for what I have to do. [*Stands up.*] I have to free myself first and those that are near me. The love of God is a very terrible thing!

> [THOMAS *tries to stop him, but is prevented by tinkers.* MARTIN *takes a wisp of straw and lights it.*]

We will destroy all that can perish! It is only the soul that can suffer no injury. The soul of man is of the imperishable substance of the stars!

> [*He throws his wisp into the heap. It blazes up.*]

ACT III

SCENE: *Before dawn a few hours later. A wild, rocky place.* NANNY *and* BIDDY LALLY *squatting by fire. Rich stuffs, etc., strewn about.* PAUDEEN *sitting, watching by* MARTIN, *who is lying, as if dead, a sack over him.*

NANNY [*to* PAUDEEN]. Well, you are great heroes and great warriors and great lads altogether to have put down the Browns the way you did, yourselves and the Whiteboys of the quarry. To have ransacked the house and have plundered it! Look at the silks and the satins and the grandeurs I brought away! Look at that now! [*Holds up a velvet cloak.*] It's a good little jacket for myself will come out of it. It's the singers will be stopping their songs and the jobbers turning from their cattle in the fairs to be taking a view of the laces of it and the buttons! It's my far-off cousins will be drawing from far and near!

BIDDY. There was not so much gold in it all as what they were saying there was. Or maybe that fleet of Whiteboys had the place ransacked before we ourselves came in. Bad cess to them that put it in my mind to go gather up the full of my bag of horseshoes out of the forge. Silver they were saying they were, pure white silver; and what are they in the end but only hardened iron! A bad end to them! [*Flings away horseshoes.*] The time I will go robbing big houses again it will not be in the light of the full moon I will go doing it, that does be causing every common thing to shine out as if for a deceit and a mockery. It's not shining at all they are at this time, but duck yellow and dark.

NANNY. To leave the big house blazing after us, it was that crowned all! Two houses to be burned to ashes in the one night. It is likely the servant-girls were rising from the feathers, and the cocks crowing from the rafters for seven miles around, taking the flames to be the whitening of the dawn.

BIDDY. It is the lad is stretched beyond you have to be thankful to for that. There was never seen a leader was his equal for spirit and for daring! Making a great scatter of the guards the way he did! Running up roofs and ladders, the fire in his hand, till you'd think he would be apt to strike his head against the stars.

NANNY. I partly guessed death was near him, and the queer shining look he had in his two eyes, and he throwing sparks east and west through the beams. I wonder now was it some inward wound he got, or did some hardy lad of the Browns give him a tip on the skull unknownst in the fight? It was I myself found him, and the troop of the Whiteboys gone, and he lying by the side of a wall as weak as if he had knocked a mountain. I failed to waken him, trying him with the sharpness of my nails, and his head fell back when I moved it, and I knew him to be spent and gone.

BIDDY. It's a pity you not to have left him where he was lying, and said no word at all to Paudeen or to that son you have, that kept us back from following on, bringing him here to this shelter on sacks and upon poles.

NANNY. What way could I help letting a screech out of myself and the life but just gone out of him in the darkness, and not a living Christian by his side but myself and the great God?

BIDDY. It's on ourselves the vengeance of the red soldiers will fall, they to find us sitting here the same as hares in a tuft. It would be best for us follow after the rest of the army of the Whiteboys.

NANNY. Whist, I tell you! The lads are cracked about him. To get but the wind of the word of leaving him, it's little but they'd knock the head off the two of us. Whist!

[*Enter* JOHNNY B. *with candles.*]

JOHNNY B. [*standing over* MARTIN]. Wouldn't you say now there was some malice or some venom in the air, that is striking down one after the other the

34

whole of the heroes of the Gael?

PAUDEEN. It makes a person be thinking of the four last ends, death and judgment, heaven and hell. Indeed and indeed my heart lies with him. It is well I knew what man he was under his by-name and his disguise. [*Sings.*]

> Oh, Johnny Gibbons, it's you were the prop to us!

> You to have left us we are put astray!

JOHNNY B. It is lost we are now and broken to the end of our days. There is no satisfaction at all but to be destroying the English; and where now will we get so good a leader again? Lay him out fair and straight upon a stone, till I will let loose the secret of my heart keening him! [*Sets out candles on a rack, propping them with stones.*]

NANNY. Is it mould candles you have brought to set around him, Johnny Bacach? It is great riches you should have in your pocket to be going to those lengths and not to be content with dips.

JOHNNY B. It is lengths I will not be going to the time the life will be gone out of your own body. It is not your corpse I will be wishful to hold in honour the way I hold this corpse in honour.

NANNY. That's the way always: there will be grief and quietness in the house if it is a young person has died, but funning and springing and tricking one another if it is an old person's corpse is in it. There is no compassion at all for the old.

PAUDEEN. It is he would have got leave for the Gael to be as high as the Gall. Believe me, he was in the prophecies. Let you not be comparing yourself with the like of him.

NANNY. Why wouldn't I be comparing myself? Look at all that was against me in the world; would you be matching me against a man of his sort that had the people shouting for him and that had nothing to do but to die and to go to heaven?

JOHNNY B. The day you go to heaven that you may never come back alive out of it! But it is not yourself will ever hear the saints hammering at their musics! It is you will be moving through the ages chains upon you, and you in the form of a dog or a monster! I tell you, that one will go through purgatory as quick as lightning through a thorn bush.

NANNY. That's the way, that's the way:

Three that are watching my time to run

The worm, the devil, and my son.

To see a loop around their neck

It's that would make my heart to leap!

JOHNNY B. Five white candles. I wouldn't begrudge them to him, indeed. If he had held out and held up, it is my belief he would have freed Ireland!

PAUDEEN. Wait till the full light of the day and you'll see the burying he'll have. It is not in this place we will be waking him. I'll make a call to the two hundred Ribbons he was to lead on to the attack on the barracks at Aughanish. They will bring him marching to his grave upon the hill. He had surely some gift from the other world, I wouldn't say but he had power from the other side.

ANDREW [*coming in, very shaky*]. Well, it was a great night he gave to the village, and it is long till it will be forgotten. I tell you the whole of the neighbours are up against him. There is no one at all this morning to set the mills going. There was no bread baked in the night-time; the horses are not fed in the stalls; the cows are not milked in the sheds. I met no man able to make a curse this night but he put it on my own head and on the head of the boy that is lying there before us…. Is there no sign of life in him at all?

JOHNNY B. What way would there be a sign of life and the life gone out of him this three hours or more?

ANDREW. He was lying in his sleep for a while yesterday, and he wakened again after another while.

NANNY. He will not waken. I tell you I held his hand in my own and it getting cold as if you were pouring on it the coldest cold water, and no running in his blood. He is gone sure enough, and the life is gone out of him.

ANDREW. Maybe so, maybe so. It seems to me yesterday his cheeks were bloomy all the while, and now he is as pale as wood-ashes. Sure we all must come to it at the last. Well, my white-headed darling, it is you were the bush among us all, and you to be cut down in your prime. Gentle and simple, everyone liked you. It is no narrow heart you had; it is you were for spending and not for getting. It is you made a good wake for yourself, scattering your estate in one night only in beer and in wine for the whole province; and that you may be sitting in the middle of paradise and in the chair of the graces!

JOHNNY B. Amen to that. It's pity I didn't think the time I sent for yourself to send the little lad of a messenger looking for a priest to overtake him. It might be in the end the Almighty is the best man for us all!

ANDREW. Sure I sent him on myself to bid the priest to come. Living or dead, I would wish to do all that is rightful for the last and the best of my own race and generation.

BIDDY [*jumping up*]. Is it the priest you are bringing in among us? Where is the sense in that? Aren't we robbed enough up to this with the expense of the candles and the like?

JOHNNY B. If it is that poor, starved priest he called to that came talking in secret signs to the man that is gone, it is likely he will ask nothing for what he has to do. There is many a priest is a Whiteboy in his heart.

NANNY. I tell you, if you brought him tied in a bag he would not say an Our Father for you, without you having a half crown at the top of your fingers.

BIDDY. There is no priest is any good at all but a spoiled priest; a one that would take a drop of drink, it is he would have courage to face the hosts of trouble. Rout them out he would, the same as a shoal of fish from out the weeds. It's best not to vex a priest, or to run against them at all.

NANNY. It's yourself humbled yourself well to one the time you were sick in the gaol and had like to die, and he bade you to give over the throwing of the cups.

BIDDY. Ah, plaster of Paris I gave him. I took to it again and I free upon the roads.

NANNY. Much good you are doing with it to yourself or any other one. Aren't you after telling that corpse no later than yesterday that he was coming within the best day of his life?

JOHNNY B. Whist, let ye! Here is the priest coming.

[FATHER JOHN *comes in.*]

FATHER JOHN. It is surely not true that he is dead?

JOHNNY B. The spirit went from him about the middle hour of the night. We brought him here to this sheltered place. We were loth to leave him without friends.

FATHER JOHN. Where is he?

JOHNNY B. [*taking up sacks*]. Lying there, stiff and stark. He has a very quiet look, as if there was no sin at all or no great trouble upon his mind.

FATHER JOHN [*kneels and touches him*]. He is not dead.

BIDDY [*pointing to* NANNY]. He is dead. If it was letting on he was, he would not have let that one rob him and search him the way she did.

FATHER JOHN. It has the appearance of death, but it is not death. He is in a trance.

PAUDEEN. Is it heaven and hell he is walking at this time to be bringing back newses of the sinners in pain?

BIDDY. I was thinking myself it might away he was, riding on white horses with the riders of the forths.

JOHNNY B. He will have great wonders to tell out the time he will rise up from the ground. It is a pity he not to waken at this time and to lead us on to overcome the troop of the English. Sure those that are in a trance get strength that they can walk on water.

ANDREW. It was Father John wakened him yesterday the time he was lying in the same way. Wasn't I telling you it was for that I called to him?

BIDDY. Waken him now till they'll see did I tell any lie in my foretelling. I knew well by the signs he was coming within the best day of his life.

PAUDEEN. And not dead at all! We'll be marching to attack Dublin itself within a week. The horn will blow for him, and all good men will gather to him. Hurry on, Father, and waken him.

FATHER JOHN. I will not waken him. I will not bring him back from where he is.

JOHNNY B. And how long will it be before he will waken of himself?

FATHER JOHN. Maybe to-day, maybe to-morrow; it is hard to be certain.

BIDDY. If it is *away* he is, he might be away seven years. To be lying like a stump of a tree and using no food and the world not able to knock a word out of him, I know the signs of it well.

JOHNNY B. We cannot be waiting and watching through seven years. If the business he has started is to be done, we have to go on here and now. The time there is any delay, that is the time the Government will get information. Waken him now, Father, and you'll get the blessing of the generations.

FATHER JOHN. I will not bring him back. God will bring him back in His own good time. For all I know he may be seeing the hidden things of God.

JOHNNY B. He might slip away in his dream. It is best to raise him up now.

ANDREW. Waken him, Father John. I thought he was surely dead this time; and what way could I go face Thomas through all that is left of my lifetime after me standing up to face him the way I did? And if I do take a little drop of an odd night, sure I'd be very lonesome if I did not take it. All the world knows it's not for love of what I drink, but for love of the people that do be with me! Waken him, Father, or maybe I would waken him myself. [*Shakes him.*]

FATHER JOHN. Lift your hand from touching him. Leave him to himself and to the power of God.

JOHNNY B. If you will not bring him back, why wouldn't we ourselves do it? Go on now, it is best for you to do it yourself.

FATHER JOHN. I woke him yesterday. He was angry with me; he could not get to the heart of the command.

JOHNNY B. If he did not, he got a command from myself that satisfied him, and a message.

FATHER JOHN. He did ... he took it from you ... and how do I know what devil's message it may have been that brought him into that devil's work, destruction and drunkenness and burnings! That was not a message from heaven! It was I awoke him; it was I kept him from hearing what was maybe a divine message, a voice of truth; and he heard you speak, and he believed the message was brought by you. You have made use of your deceit and his mistaking ... you have left him without house or means to support him, you are striving to destroy and to drag him to entire ruin. I will not help you, I would rather see him die in his trance and go into God's hands than awake him and see him go into hell's mouth with vagabonds and outcasts like you!

JOHNNY B. [*turning to* BIDDY]. You should have knowledge, Biddy Lally, of the means to bring back a man that is away.

BIDDY. The power of the earth will do it through its herbs, and the power of the air will do it kindling fire into flame.

JOHNNY B. Rise up and make no delay. Stretch out and gather a handful of an herb that will bring him back from whatever place he is in.

BIDDY. Where is the use of herbs and his teeth clenched the way he could not use them?

JOHNNY B. Take fire so in the devil's name and put it to the soles of his feet. [*Takes lighted sod from fire.*]

FATHER JOHN. Let him alone, I say!

[*Dashes away the sod.*]

JOHNNY B. I will not leave him alone! I will not give in to leave him swooning there and the country waiting for him to awake!

FATHER JOHN. I tell you I awoke him! I sent him into thieves' company! I will not have him wakened again and evil things, it may be, waiting to take hold of him! Back from him, back, I say! Will you dare to lay a hand on me? You cannot do it! You cannot touch him against my will!

BIDDY. Mind yourself; don't be bringing us under the curse of the church.

[JOHNNY *falls back.* MARTIN *moves.*]

FATHER JOHN. It is God has him in His care. It is He is awaking him. [MARTIN *has risen to his elbow.*] Do not touch him, do not speak to him, he may be hearing great secrets.

MARTIN. That music, I must go nearer … sweet, marvellous music … louder than the trampling of the unicorns … far louder, though the mountain is shaking with their feet … high, joyous music.

FATHER JOHN. Hush, he is listening to the music of heaven!

MARTIN. Take me to you, musicians, wherever you are! I will go nearer to you; I hear you better now, more and more joyful; that is strange, it is strange.

FATHER JOHN. He is getting some secret.

MARTIN. It is the music of paradise, that is certain, somebody said that. It is certainly the music of paradise. Ah, now I hear, now I understand. It is made of the continual clashing of swords!

JOHNNY B. That is the best music. We will clash them sure enough. We will clash our swords and our pikes on the bayonets of the red soldiers. It is well you rose up from the dead to lead us! Come on now, come on!

MARTIN. Who are you? Ah, I remember…. Where are you asking me to come to?

PAUDEEN. To come on, to be sure, to the attack on the barracks at Aughanish.

To carry on the work you took in hand last night.

MARTIN. What work did I take in hand last night? Oh, yes, I remember ... some big house ... we burned it down.... But I had not understood the vision when I did that. I had not heard the command right. That was not the work I was sent to do.

PAUDEEN. Rise up now and bid us what to do. Your great name itself will clear the road before you. It is you yourself will have freed all Ireland before the stooks will be in stacks!

MARTIN. Listen, I will explain ... I have misled you. It is only now I have the whole vision plain. As I lay there I saw through everything, I know all. It was but a frenzy, that going out to burn and to destroy. What have I to do with the foreign army? What I have to pierce is the wild heart of time. My business is not reformation but revelation.

JOHNNY B. If you are going to turn back now from leading us, you are no better than any other traitor that ever gave up the work he took in hand. Let you come and face now the two hundred men you brought out, daring the power of the law last night, and give them your reason for failing them.

MARTIN. I was mistaken when I set out to destroy church and law. The battle we have to fight is fought out in our own minds. There is a fiery moment, perhaps once in a lifetime, and in that moment we see the only thing that matters. It is in that moment the great battles are lost and won, for in that moment we are a part of the host of heaven.

PAUDEEN. Have you betrayed us to the naked hangman with your promises and with your drink? If you brought us out here to fail us and to ridicule us, it is the last day you will live!

JOHNNY B. The curse of my heart on you! It would be right to send you to your own place on the flagstone of the traitors in hell. When once I have made an end of you, I will be as well satisfied to be going to my death for it as if I was going home!

MARTIN. Father John, Father John, can you not hear? Can you not see? Are you blind? Are you deaf?

FATHER JOHN. What is it? What is it?

MARTIN. There on the mountain, a thousand white unicorns trampling; a thousand riders with their swords drawn ... the swords clashing! Oh, the sound of the swords, the sound of the clashing of the swords! [*He goes slowly off stage.*]

[JOHNNY B. *takes up a stone to throw at him.*]

FATHER JOHN [*seizing his arm*]. Stop ... do you not see he is beyond the world?

BIDDY. Keep your hand off him, Johnny Bacach. If he is gone wild and cracked, that's natural. Those that have been wakened from a trance on a sudden are apt to go bad and light in the head.

PAUDEEN. If it is madness is on him, it is not he himself should pay the penalty.

BIDDY. To prey on the mind it does, and rises into the head. There are some would go over any height and would have great power in their madness. It is maybe to some secret cleft he is going to get knowledge of the great cure for all things, or of the Plough that was hidden in the old times, the Golden Plough.

PAUDEEN. It seemed as if he was talking through honey. He had the look of one that had seen great wonders. It is maybe among the old heroes of Ireland he went raising armies for our help.

FATHER JOHN. God take him in His care and keep him from lying spirits and from all delusions.

JOHNNY B. We have got candles here, Father. We had them to put around his body. Maybe they would keep away the evil things of the air.

Paudeen. Light them so, and he will say out a Mass for him the same as in a lime-washed church.

[*They light the candles on the rock.* THOMAS *comes in.*]

THOMAS. Where is he? I am come to warn him. The destruction he did in the night-time has been heard of. The soldiers are out after him and the constables ... there are two of the constables not far off ... there are others on every side ... they heard he was here in the mountain ... where is he?

FATHER JOHN. He has gone up the path.

THOMAS. Hurry after him! Tell him to hide himself ... this attack he had a hand in is a hanging crime.... Tell him to hide himself, to come to me when all is quiet ... bad as his doings are, he is my own brother's son; I will get him on to a ship that will be going to France.

FATHER JOHN. That will be best; send him back to the Brothers and to the wise Bishops. They can unravel this tangle. I cannot; I cannot be sure of the truth.

THOMAS. Here are the constables; he will see them and get away.... Say no word.... The Lord be praised that he is out of sight.

> [CONSTABLES *come in.*]

CONSTABLE. The man we are looking for, where is he? He was seen coming here along with you. You have to give him up into the power of the law.

JOHNNY B. We will not give him up! Go back out of this or you will be sorry.

PAUDEEN. We are not in dread of you or the like of you.

BIDDY. Throw them down over the rocks!

NANNY. Give them to the picking of the crows!

ALL. Down with the law!

FATHER JOHN. Hush! He is coming back. [*To* CONSTABLES.] Stop, stop ... leave him to himself. He is not trying to escape; he is coming towards you.

PAUDEEN. There is a sort of a brightness about him. I misjudged him calling him a traitor. It is not to this world he belongs at all. He is over on the other side.

> [MARTIN *has come in. He stands higher than the others upon some rocks.*]

MARTIN. *Ex calix meus inebrians quam praeclarus est!*

FATHER JOHN. I must know what he has to say. It is not from himself he is speaking.

MARTIN. Father John, heaven is not what we have believed it to be. It is not quiet; it is not singing and making music and all strife at an end. I have seen it, I have been there. The lover still loves, but with a greater passion; and the rider still rides, but the horse goes like the wind and leaps the ridges; and the battle goes on always, always. That is the joy of heaven, continual battle. I thought the battle was here, and that the joy was to be found here on earth, that all one had to do was to bring again the old, wild earth of the stories, but no, it is not here; we shall not come to that joy, that battle, till we have put out the senses, everything that can be seen and handled, as I put out this candle.

43

[*He puts out candle.*] We must put out the whole world as I put out this candle [*he puts out candle*]; we must put out the light of the stars and the light of the sun and the light of the moon [*he puts out the remaining candles and comes down to where the others are*], till we have brought everything to nothing once again. I saw in a broken vision, but now all is clear to me. Where there is nothing, where there is nothing ... there is God!

CONSTABLE. Now we will take him!

JOHNNY B. We will never give him up to the law!

PAUDEEN. Make your escape! We will not let you be followed.

> [*They struggle with* CONSTABLES; *the women help them; all disappear, struggling. There is a shot.* MARTIN *falls dead. Beggars come back with a shout.*]

JOHNNY B. We have done for them; they will not meddle with you again.

PAUDEEN. Oh, he is down!

FATHER JOHN. He is shot through the breast. Oh, who has dared meddle with a soul that was in the tumults on the threshold of sanctity?

JOHNNY B. It was that gun went off and I striking it from the constable's hand.

MARTIN [*looking at his hand, on which there is blood*]. Ah, that is blood! I fell among the rocks. It is a hard climb. It is a long climb to the vineyards of Eden. Help me up. I must go on. The Mountain of Abiegnos is very high ... but the vineyards ... the vineyards!

> [*He falls back, dead. The men uncover their heads.*]

PAUDEEN [*to* BIDDY]. It was you misled him with your foretelling that he was coming within the best day of his life.

JOHNNY B. Madness on him or no madness, I will not leave that body to the law to be buried with a dog's burial or brought away and maybe hanged upon a tree. Lift him on the sacks; bring him away to the quarry; it is there on the hillside the boys will give him a great burying, coming on horses and bearing white rods in their hands.

> [*They lift him and carry the body away, singing.*]

Our hope and our darling, our heart dies with you.

You to have failed us, we are foals astray!

FATHER JOHN. He is gone, and we can never know where that vision came from. I cannot know; the wise Bishops would have known.

THOMAS [*taking up banner*]. To be shaping a lad through his lifetime, and he to go his own way at the last, and a queer way. It is very queer the world itself is, whatever shape was put upon it at the first!

ANDREW. To be too headstrong and too open, that is the beginning of trouble. To keep to yourself the thing that you know, and to do in quiet the thing you want to do, there would be no disturbance at all in the world, all people to bear that in mind!

CURTAIN

CATHLEEN NI HOULIHAN

CHARACTERS

PETER GILLANE.

MICHAEL GILLANE   *his son, going to be married.*

PATRICK GILLANE   *a lad of twelve, Michael's brother.*

BRIDGET GILLANE   *Peter's wife.*

DELIA CAHEL   *engaged to* MICHAEL.

THE POOR OLD WOMAN.

NEIGHBOURS.

SCENE: *Interior of a cottage close to Killala, in 1798.* BRIDGET *is standing at a table undoing a parcel.* PETER *is sitting at one side of the fire,* PATRICK *at the other.*

PETER. What is that sound I hear?

PATRICK. I don't hear anything. [*He listens.*] I hear it now. It's like cheering. [*He goes to the window and looks out.*] I wonder what they are cheering about. I don't see anybody.

PETER. It might be a hurling match.

PATRICK. There's no hurling to-day. It must be down in the town the cheering is.

BRIDGET. I suppose the boys must be having some sport of their own. Come over here, Peter, and look at Michael's wedding-clothes.

PETER [*shifts his chair to table*]. Those are grand clothes, indeed.

BRIDGET. You hadn't clothes like that when you married me, and no coat to put on of a Sunday any more than any other day.

PETER. That is true, indeed. We never thought a son of our own would be wearing a suit of that sort for his wedding, or have so good a place to bring a wife to.

PATRICK [*who is still at the window*]. There's an old woman coming down the road. I don't know, is it here she's coming?

BRIDGET. It will be a neighbour coming to hear about Michael's wedding. Can you see who it is?

PATRICK. I think it is a stranger, but she's not coming to the house. She's turned into the gap that goes down where Murteen and his sons are shearing sheep. [*He turns towards* BRIDGET.] Do you remember what Winny of the Cross Roads was saying the other night about the strange woman that goes through the country whatever time there's war or trouble coming?

BRIDGET. Don't be bothering us about Winny's talk, but go and open the door for your brother. I hear him coming up the path.

PETER. I hope he has brought Delia's fortune with him safe, for fear her people might go back on the bargain and I after making it. Trouble enough I had making it.

[PATRICK *opens the door and* MICHAEL *comes in.*]

BRIDGET. What kept you, Michael? We were looking out for you this long time.

MICHAEL. I went round by the priest's house to bid him be ready to marry us to-morrow.

BRIDGET. Did he say anything?

MICHAEL. He said it was a very nice match, and that he was never better pleased to marry any two in his parish than myself and Delia Cahel.

PETER. Have you got the fortune, Michael?

MICHAEL. Here it is.

[*He puts bag on table and goes over and leans against the chimney-jamb.* BRIDGET, *who has been all this time examining the clothes, pulling the seams and trying the lining of the pockets, etc., puts the clothes on the dresser.*]

PETER [*getting up and taking the bag in his hand and turning out the money*]. Yes, I made the bargain well for you, Michael. Old John Cahel would sooner have kept a share of this awhile longer. "Let me keep the half of it till the first boy is born," says he. "You will not," says I. "Whether there is or is not a boy, the whole hundred pounds must be in Michael's hands before he brings your daughter in the house." The wife spoke to him then, and he gave in at the end.

BRIDGET. You seem well pleased to be handling the money, Peter.

PETER. Indeed, I wish I had had the luck to get a hundred pounds, or twenty pounds itself, with the wife I married.

BRIDGET. Well, if I didn't bring much I didn't get much. What had you the day I married you but a flock of hens and you feeding them, and a few lambs and you driving them to the market at Ballina? [*She is vexed and bangs a jug on the dresser.*] If I brought no fortune, I worked it out in my bones, laying down the baby, Michael that is standing there now, on a stook of straw, while I dug the potatoes, and never asking big dresses or anything but to be working.

PETER. That is true, indeed. [*He pats her arm.*]

BRIDGET. Leave me alone now till I ready the house for the woman that is to come into it.

PETER. You are the best woman in Ireland, but money is good, too. [*He begins handling the money again and sits down.*] I never thought to see so much money within my four walls. We can do great things now we have it. We can take the ten acres of land we have a chance of since Jamsie Dempsey died, and stock it. We will go to the fair of Ballina to buy the stock. Did Delia ask any of the money for her own use, Michael?

MICHAEL. She did not, indeed. She did not seem to take much notice of it, or to look at it at all.

BRIDGET. That's no wonder. Why would she look at it when she had yourself to look at, a fine, strong young man? It is proud she must be to get you, a good steady boy that will make use of the money, and not be running through it or spending it on drink like another.

PETER. It's likely Michael himself was not thinking much of the fortune either, but of what sort the girl was to look at.

MICHAEL [*coming over towards the table*]. Well, you would like a nice comely girl to be beside you, and to go walking with you. The fortune only lasts for a while, but the woman will be there always.

[*Cheers.*]

PATRICK [*turning round from the window*]. They are cheering again down in the town. Maybe they are landing horses from Enniscrone. They do be cheering when the horses take the water well.

MICHAEL. There are no horses in it. Where would they be going and no fair at hand? Go down to the town, Patrick, and see what is going on.

PATRICK [*opens the door to go out, but stops for a moment on the threshold*]. Will Delia remember, do you think, to bring the greyhound pup she promised me when she would be coming to the house?

MICHAEL. She will surely.

[PATRICK *goes out, leaving the door open.*]

PETER. It will be Patrick's turn next to be looking for a fortune, but he won't find it so easy to get it and he with no place of his own.

BRIDGET. I do be thinking sometimes, now things are going so well with us, and the Cahels such a good back to us in the district, and Delia's own uncle a priest, we might be put in the way of making Patrick a priest some day, and he so good at his books.

PETER. Time enough, time enough; you have always your head full of plans, Bridget.

BRIDGET. We will be well able to give him learning, and not to send him trampling the country like a poor scholar that lives on charity.

[*Cheers.*]

MICHAEL. They're not done cheering yet.

[*He goes over to the door and stands there for a moment, putting up his hand to shade his eyes.*]

BRIDGET. Do you see anything?

MICHAEL. I see an old woman coming up the path.

BRIDGET. Who is it, I wonder. It must be the strange woman Patrick saw awhile ago.

MICHAEL. I don't think it's one of the neighbours anyway, but she has her cloak over her face.

BRIDGET. It might be some poor woman heard we were making ready for the wedding and came to look for her share.

PETER. I may as well put the money out of sight. There is no use leaving it out for every stranger to look at.

[*He goes over to a large box in the corner, opens it, and puts the*

49

bag in and fumbles at the lock.]

MICHAEL. There she is, father! [*An* Old Woman *passes the window slowly; she looks at* MICHAEL *as she passes.*] I'd sooner a stranger not to come to the house the night before my wedding.

BRIDGET. Open the door, Michael; don't keep the poor woman waiting.

[*The* OLD WOMAN *comes in.* MICHAEL *stands aside to make way for her.*]

OLD WOMAN. God save all here!

PETER. God save you kindly!

OLD WOMAN. You have good shelter here.

PETER. You are welcome to whatever shelter we have.

BRIDGET. Sit down there by the fire and welcome.

OLD WOMAN [*warming her hands*]. There is a hard wind outside.

[MICHAEL *watches her curiously from the door.* PETER *comes over to the table.*]

PETER. Have you travelled far to-day?

OLD WOMAN. I have travelled far, very far; there are few have travelled so far as myself, and there's many a one that doesn't make me welcome. There was one that had strong sons I thought were friends of mine, but they were shearing their sheep, and they wouldn't listen to me.

PETER. It's a pity indeed for any person to have no place of their own.

OLD WOMAN. That's true for you indeed, and it's long I'm on the roads since I first went wandering.

BRIDGET. It is a wonder you are not worn out with so much wandering.

OLD WOMAN. Sometimes my feet are tired and my hands are quiet, but there is no quiet in my heart. When the people see me quiet, they think old age has come on me and that all the stir has gone out of me. But when the trouble is on me I must be talking to my friends.

BRIDGET. What was it put you wandering?

OLD WOMAN. Too many strangers in the house.

BRIDGET. Indeed you look as if you'd had your share of trouble.

OLD WOMAN. I have had trouble indeed.

BRIDGET. What was it put the trouble on you?

OLD WOMAN. My land that was taken from me.

PETER. Was it much land they took from you?

OLD WOMAN. My four beautiful green fields.

PETER [*aside to* BRIDGET]. Do you think could she be the widow Casey that was put out of her holding at Kilglass awhile ago?

BRIDGET. She is not. I saw the widow Casey one time at the market in Ballina, a stout fresh woman.

PETER [*to* OLD WOMAN]. Did you hear a noise of cheering, and you coming up the hill?

OLD WOMAN. I thought I heard the noise I used to hear when my friends came to visit me. [*She begins singing half to herself.*]

> I will go cry with the woman,
>
> For yellow-haired Donough is dead,
>
> With a hempen rope for a neckcloth,
>
> And a white cloth on his head,—

MICHAEL [*coming from the door*]. What is that you are singing, ma'am?

OLD WOMAN. Singing I am about a man I knew one time, yellow-haired Donough, that was hanged in Galway. [*She goes on singing, much louder.*]

> I am come to cry with you, woman,
>
> My hair is unwound and unbound;
>
> I remember him ploughing his field,
>
> Turning up the red side of the ground,

And building his barn on the hill With the good mortared stone; O! we'd have pulled down the gallows Had it happened in Enniscrone!

MICHAEL. What was it brought him to his death?

OLD WOMAN. He died for love of me: many a man has died for love of me.

PETER [*aside to* BRIDGET]. Her trouble has put her wits astray.

MICHAEL. Is it long since that song was made? Is it long since he got his death?

OLD WOMAN. Not long, not long. But there were others that died for love of me a long time ago.

MICHAEL. Were they neighbours of your own, ma'am?

OLD WOMAN. Come here beside me and I'll tell you about them. [MICHAEL *sits down beside her at the hearth.*] There was a red man of the O'Donnells from the north, and a man of the O'Sullivans from the south, and there was one Brian that lost his life at Clontarf by the sea, and there were a great many in the west, some that died hundreds of years ago, and there are some that will die to-morrow.

MICHAEL. Is it in the west that men will die to-morrow?

OLD WOMAN. Come nearer, nearer to me.

BRIDGET. Is she right, do you think? Or is she a woman from beyond the world?

PETER. She doesn't know well what she's talking about, with the want and the trouble she has gone through.

BRIDGET. The poor thing, we should treat her well.

PETER. Give her a drink of milk and a bit of the oaten cake.

BRIDGET. Maybe we should give her something along with that, to bring her on her way. A few pence, or a shilling itself, and we with so much money in the house.

PETER. Indeed I'd not begrudge it to her if we had it to spare, but if we go running through what we have, we'll soon have to break the hundred pounds, and that would be a pity.

BRIDGET. Shame on you, Peter. Give her the shilling, and your blessing with it, or our own luck will go from us.

[PETER *goes to the box and takes out a shilling.*]

BRIDGET [*to the* OLD WOMAN]. Will you have a drink of milk?

OLD WOMAN. It is not food or drink that I want.

PETER [*offering the shilling*]. Here is something for you.

OLD WOMAN. That is not what I want. It is not silver I want.

PETER. What is it you would be asking for?

OLD WOMAN. If anyone would give me help he must give me himself, he must give me all.

[PETER *goes over to the table, staring at the shilling in his hand in a bewildered way, and stands whispering to* BRIDGET.]

MICHAEL. Have you no one to care you in your age, ma'am?

OLD WOMAN. I have not. With all the lovers that brought me their love, I never set out the bed for any.

MICHAEL. Are you lonely going the roads, ma'am? OLD

WOMAN. I have my thoughts and I have my hopes.

MICHAEL. What hopes have you to hold to?

OLD WOMAN. The hope of getting my beautiful fields back again; the hope of putting the strangers out of my house.

MICHAEL. What way will you do that, ma'am?

OLD WOMAN. I have good friends that will help me. They are gathering to help me now. I am not afraid. If they are put down to-day, they will get the upper hand to-morrow. [*She gets up.*] I must be going to meet my friends. They are coming to help me, and I must be there to welcome them. I must call the neighbours together to welcome them.

MICHAEL. I will go with you.

BRIDGET. It is not her friends you have to go and welcome, Michael; it is the girl coming into the house you have to welcome. You have plenty to do, it is food and drink you have to bring to the house. The woman that is coming home is not coming with empty hands; you would not have an empty house before her. [*To the* OLD WOMAN.] Maybe you don't know, ma'am, that my son is going to be married to-morrow.

OLD WOMAN. It is not a man going to his marriage that I look to for help.

PETER [*to* BRIDGET]. Who is she, do you think, at all?

BRIDGET. You did not tell us your name yet, ma'am.

OLD WOMAN. Some call me the Poor Old Woman, and there are some that call me Cathleen, the daughter of Houlihan.

PETER. I think I knew someone of that name once. Who was it, I wonder? It must have been someone I knew when I was a boy. No, no, I remember, I heard it in a song.

OLD WOMAN [*who is standing in the doorway*]. They are wondering that there were songs made for me; there have been many songs made for me. I heard one on the wind this morning. [*She sings.*]

Do not make a great keening When the graves have been dug to-morrow. Do not call the white-scarfed riders To the burying that shall be to-morrow.

Do not spread food to call strangers To the wakes that shall be to-morrow; Do not give money for prayers For the dead that shall die to-morrow …

they will have no need of prayers, they will have no need of prayers.

MICHAEL. I do not know what that song means, but tell me something I can do for you.

PETER. Come over to me, Michael.

MICHAEL. Hush, father, listen to her.

OLD WOMAN. It is a hard service they take that help me. Many that are red-cheeked now will be pale-cheeked; many that have been free to walk the hills and the bogs and the rushes will be sent to walk hard streets in far countries; many a good plan will be broken; many that have gathered money will not stay to spend it; many a child will be born, and there will be no father at its christening to give it a name. They that had red cheeks will have pale cheeks for my sake; and for all that, they will think they are well paid.

[*She goes out; her voice is heard outside singing.*]

They shall be remembered for ever, They shall be alive for ever, They shall be speaking for ever, The people shall hear them for ever.

BRIDGET [*to* PETER]. Look at him, Peter; he has the look of a man that has got the touch. [*Raising her voice.*] Look here, Michael, at the wedding-clothes. Such grand clothes as these are. You have a right to fit them on now; it would be a pity to-morrow if they did not fit. The boys would be laughing at you. Take them, Michael, and go into the room and fit them on. [*She puts them on his arm.*]

MICHAEL. What wedding are you talking of? What clothes will I be wearing to-morrow?

BRIDGET. These are the clothes you are going to wear when you marry Delia

Cahel to-morrow.

MICHAEL. I had forgotten that.

> [*He looks at the clothes and turns towards the inner room, but stops at the sound of cheering outside.*]

PETER. There is the shouting come to our own door. What is it has happened?

> [PATRICK *and* DELIA *come in.*]

PATRICK. There are ships in the Bay; the French are landing at Killala!

> [PETER *takes his pipe from his mouth and his hat off, and stands up. The clothes slip from* MICHAEL's *arm.*]

DELIA. Michael! [*He takes no notice.*] Michael! [*He turns towards her.*] Why do you look at me like a stranger?

> [*She drops his arm.* BRIDGET *goes over towards her.*]

PATRICK. The boys are all hurrying down the hillsides to join the French.

DELIA. Michael won't be going to join the French.

BRIDGET [*to* PETER]. Tell him not to go, Peter.

PETER. It's no use. He doesn't hear a word we're saying.

BRIDGET. Try and coax him over to the fire.

DELIA. Michael! Michael! You won't leave me! You won't join the French, and we going to be married!

> [*She puts her arms about him; he turns towards her as if about to yield.* OLD WOMAN's *voice outside.*]

They shall be speaking for ever, The people shall hear them for ever.

> [MICHAEL *breaks away from* DELIA *and goes out.*]

PETER [*to* PATRICK, *laying a hand on his arm*]. Did you see an old woman going down the path?

PATRICK. I did not, but I saw a young girl, and she had the walk of a queen.

THE HOUR-GLASS:

A MORALITY

CHARACTERS

A WISE MAN.	SOME PUPILS.
A FOOL.	AN ANGEL.
THE WISE MAN'S WIFE AND TWO CHILDREN.	

SCENE: *A large room with a door at the back and another at the side or else a curtained place where the persons can enter by parting the curtains. A desk and a chair at one side. An hour-glass on a stand near the door. A creepy stool near it. Some benches. A* WISE MAN *sitting at his desk.*

WISE M. [*turning over the pages of a book*]. Where is that passage I am to explain to my pupils to-day? Here it is, and the book says that it was written by a beggar on the walls of Babylon: "There are two living countries, the one visible and the one invisible; and when it is winter with us it is summer in that country, and when the November winds are up among us it is lambing time there." I wish that my pupils had asked me to explain any other passage. [*The* FOOL *comes in and stands at the door holding out his hat. He has a pair of shears in the other hand.*] It sounds to me like foolishness; and yet that cannot be, for the writer of this book, where I have found so much knowledge, would not have set it by itself on this page, and surrounded it with so many images and so many deep colours and so much fine gilding, if it had been foolishness.

FOOL. Give me a penny.

WISE M. [*turns to another page*]. Here he has written: "The learned in old times forgot the visible country." That I understand, but I have taught my learners better.

FOOL. Won't you give me a penny?

WISE M. What do you want? The words of the wise Saracen will not teach you much.

FOOL. Such a great wise teacher as you are will not refuse a penny to a Fool.

WISE M. What do you know about wisdom?

FOOL. Oh, I know! I know what I have seen.

WISE M. What is it you have seen?

FOOL. When I went by Kilcluan where the bells used to be ringing at the break of every day, I could hear nothing but the people snoring in their houses. When I went by Tubbervanach where the young men used to be climbing the hill to the blessed well, they were sitting at the crossroads playing cards. When I went by Carrigoras, where the friars used to be fasting and serving the poor, I saw them drinking wine and obeying their wives. And when I asked what misfortune had brought all these changes, they said it was no misfortune, but it was the wisdom they had learned from your teaching.

WISE M. Run round to the kitchen, and my wife will give you something to eat.

FOOL. That is foolish advice for a wise man to give.

WISE M. Why, Fool?

FOOL. What is eaten is gone. I want pennies for my bag. I must buy bacon in the shops, and nuts in the market, and strong drink for the time when the sun is weak. And I want snares to catch the rabbits and the squirrels and the hares, and a pot to cook them in.

WISE M. Go away. I have other things to think of now than giving you pennies.

FOOL. Give me a penny and I will bring you luck. Bresal the Fisherman lets me sleep among the nets in his loft in the winter-time because he says I bring him luck; and in the summer-time the wild creatures let me sleep near their nests and their holes. It is lucky even to look at me or to touch me, but it is much more lucky to give me a penny. [*Holds out his hand.*] If I wasn't lucky, I'd starve.

WISE M. What have you got the shears for?

FOOL. I won't tell you. If I told you, you would drive them away.

WISE M. Whom would I drive away?

FOOL. I won't tell you.

WISE M. Not if I give you a penny?

FOOL. No.

WISE M. Not if I give you two pennies?

FOOL. You will be very lucky if you give me two pennies, but I won't tell you!

WISE M. Three pennies?

FOOL. Four, and I will tell you!

WISE M. Very well, four. But I will not call you Teigue the Fool any longer.

FOOL. Let me come close to you where nobody will hear me. But first you must promise you will not drive them away. [WISE M. *nods.*] Every day men go out dressed in black and spread great black nets over the hills, great black nets.

WISE M. Why do they do that?

FOOL. That they may catch the feet of the angels. But every morning, just before the dawn, I go out and cut the nets with my shears, and the angels fly away.

WISE M. Ah, now I know that you are Teigue the Fool. You have told me that I am wise, and I have never seen an angel.

FOOL. I have seen plenty of angels.

WISE M. Do you bring luck to the angels too?

FOOL. Oh, no, no! No one could do that. But they are always there if one looks about one; they are like the blades of grass.

WISE M. When do you see them?

FOOL. When one gets quiet, then something wakes up inside one, something happy and quiet like the stars—not like the seven that move, but like the fixed stars. [*He points upward.*]

WISE M. And what happens then?

FOOL. Then all in a minute one smells summer flowers, and tall people go by, happy and laughing, and their clothes are the colour of burning sods.

WISE M. Is it long since you have seen them, Teigue the Fool?

FOOL. Not long, glory be to God! I saw one coming behind me just now. It was not laughing, but it had clothes the colour of burning sods, and there was something shining about its head.

W_{ISE} M. Well, there are your four pennies. You, a fool, say "glory be to God," but before I came the wise men said it.

F_{OOL}. Four pennies! That means a great deal of luck. Great teacher, I have brought you plenty of luck!

[*He goes out shaking the bag.*]

W_{ISE} M. Though they call him Teigue the Fool, he is not more foolish than everybody used to be, with their dreams and their preachings and their three worlds; but I have overthrown their three worlds with the seven sciences. [*He touches the books with his hands.*] With Philosophy that was made from the lonely star, I have taught them to forget Theology; with Architecture, I have hidden the ramparts of their cloudy heaven; with Music, the fierce planets' daughter whose hair is always on fire, and with Grammar that is the moon's daughter, I have shut their ears to the imaginary harpings and speech of the angels; and I have made formations of battle with Arithmetic that have put the hosts of heaven to the rout. But, Rhetoric and Dialectic, that have been born out of the light star and out of the amorous star, you have been my spear-man and my catapult! Oh! my swift horsemen! Oh! my keen darting arguments, it is because of you that I have overthrown the hosts of foolishness! [*An* Angel, *in a dress the colour of embers, and carrying a blossoming apple bough in her hand and a gilded halo about her head, stands upon the threshold.*] Before I came, men's minds were stuffed with folly about a heaven where birds sang the hours, and about angels that came and stood upon men's thresholds. But I have locked the visions into heaven and turned the key upon them. Well, I must consider this passage about the two countries. My mother used to say something of the kind. She would say that when our bodies sleep our souls awake, and that whatever withers here ripens yonder, and that harvests are snatched from us that they may feed invisible people. But the meaning of the book may be different, for only fools and women have thoughts like that; their thoughts were never written upon the walls of Babylon. I must ring the bell for my pupils. [*He sees the* A_{NGEL}.] What are you? Who are you? I think I saw some that were like you in my dreams when I was a child—that bright thing, that dress that is the colour of embers! But I have done with dreams, I have done with dreams.

A_{NGEL}. I am the Angel of the Most High God.

W_{ISE} M. Why have you come to me?

A_{NGEL}. I have brought you a message.

W_{ISE} M. What message have you got for me?

A_{NGEL}. You will die within the hour. You will die when the last grains have fallen in this glass. [*She turns the hour-glass.*]

W_{ISE} M. My time to die has not come. I have my pupils. I have a young wife and children that I cannot leave. Why must I die?

A_{NGEL}. You must die because no souls have passed over the threshold of Heaven since you came into this country. The threshold is grassy, and the gates are rusty, and the angels that keep watch there are lonely.

W_{ISE} M. Where will death bring me to?

A_{NGEL}. The doors of Heaven will not open to you, for you have denied the existence of Heaven; and the doors of Purgatory will not open to you, for you have denied the existence of Purgatory.

W_{ISE} M. But I have also denied the existence of Hell!

A_{NGEL}. Hell is the place of those who deny.

W_{ISE} M. [*kneels*]. I have, indeed, denied everything, and have taught others to deny. I have believed in nothing but what my senses told me. But, oh! beautiful Angel, forgive me, forgive me!

A_{NGEL}. You should have asked forgiveness long ago.

W_{ISE} M. Had I seen your face as I see it now, oh! beautiful angel, I would have believed, I would have asked forgiveness. Maybe you do not know how easy it is to doubt. Storm, death, the grass rotting, many sicknesses, those are the messengers that came to me. Oh! why are you silent? You carry the pardon of the Most High; give it to me! I would kiss your hands if I were not afraid—no, no, the hem of your dress!

A_{NGEL}. You let go undying hands too long ago to take hold of them now.

W_{ISE} M. You cannot understand. You live in that country people only see in their dreams. Maybe it is as hard for you to understand why we disbelieve as it is for us to believe. Oh! what have I said! You know everything! Give me time to undo what I have done. Give me a year—a month—a day—an hour! Give me to this hour's end, that I may undo what I have done!

A_{NGEL}. You cannot undo what you have done. Yet I have this power with my message. If you can find one that believes before the hour's end, you shall come to Heaven after the years of Purgatory. For, from one fiery seed, watched over by those that sent me, the harvest can come again to heap the golden threshing floor. But now farewell, for I am weary of the weight of time.

Wise M. Blessed be the Father, blessed be the Son, blessed be the Spirit, blessed be the Messenger They have sent!

Angel [*at the door and pointing at the hour-glass*]. In a little while the uppermost glass will be empty. [*Goes out.*]

Wise M. Everything will be well with me. I will call my pupils; they only say they doubt. [*Pulls the bell.*] They will be here in a moment. They want to please me; they pretend that they disbelieve. Belief is too old to be overcome all in a minute. Besides, I can prove what I once disproved. [*Another pull at the bell.*] They are coming now. I will go to my desk. I will speak quietly, as if nothing had happened.

> [*He stands at the desk with a fixed look in his eyes. The voices of the pupils are heard outside singing these words.*]

I was going the road one day, O the brown and the yellow beer, And I met with a man that was no right man O my dear, O my dear.

> [*The sound grows louder as they come nearer, but ceases on the threshold.*]

Enter Pupils *and the* Fool.

Fool. Leave me alone. Leave me alone. Who is that pulling at my bag? King's son, do not pull at my bag.

A Young Man. Did your friends the angels give you that bag? Why don't they fill your bag for you?

Fool. Give me pennies! Give me some pennies!

A Young M. What do you want pennies for?—that great bag at your waist is heavy.

Fool. I want to buy bacon in the shops, and nuts in the market, and strong drink for the time when the sun is weak, and snares to catch rabbits and the squirrels that steal the nuts, and hares, and a great pot to cook them in.

A Young M. Why don't your friends tell you where buried treasures are? Why don't they make you dream about treasures? If one dreams three times there is always treasure.

FOOL [*holding out his hat*]. Give me pennies! Give me pennies!

> [*They throw pennies into his hat. He is standing close to the door, that he may hold out his hat to each newcomer.*]

A YOUNG M. Master, will you have Teigue the Fool for a scholar?

ANOTHER YOUNG M. Teigue, will you give us your pennies if we teach you lessons? No, he goes to school for nothing on the mountains. Tell us what you learn on the mountains, Teigue.

WISE M. Be silent all! [*He has been standing silent, looking away.*] Stand still in your places, for there is something I would have you tell me.

> [*A moment's pause. They all stand round in their places.* TEIGUE *still stands at the door.*]

WISE M. Is there anyone amongst you who believes in God? In Heaven? Or in Purgatory? Or in Hell?

ALL THE YOUNG MEN. No one, Master! No one!

WISE M. I knew you would all say that; but do not be afraid. I will not be angry. Tell me the truth. Do you not believe?

A YOUNG M. We once did, but you have taught us to know better.

WISE M. Oh, teaching! teaching does not go very deep! The heart remains unchanged under it all. You have the faith that you have always had, and you are afraid to tell me.

A YOUNG M. No, no, Master!

WISE M. If you tell me that you have not changed, I shall be glad and not angry.

A YOUNG M. [*to his* NEIGHBOUR]. He wants somebody to dispute with.

HIS NEIGHBOUR. I knew that from the beginning.

A YOUNG M. That is not the subject for to-day; you were going to talk about the words the beggar wrote upon the walls of Babylon.

WISE M. If there is one amongst you that believes, he will be my best friend. Surely there is one amongst you. [*They are all silent.*] Surely what you learned at your mother's knees has not been so soon forgotten.

A YOUNG M. Master, till you came, no teacher in this land was able to get rid of foolishness and ignorance. But every one has listened to you, every one has learned the truth. You have had your last disputation.

ANOTHER. What a fool you made of that monk in the market-place! He had not a word to say.

WISE M. [*comes from his desk and stands among them in the middle of the room*]. Pupils, dear friends, I have deceived you all this time. It was I myself who was ignorant. There is a God. There is a Heaven. There is fire that passes and there is fire that lasts for ever.

> [TEIGUE, *through all this, is sitting on a stool by the door, reckoning on his fingers what he will buy with his money.*]

A YOUNG M. [*to* Another]. He will not be satisfied till we dispute with him. [*To the* WISE MAN.] Prove it, Master. Have you seen them?

WISE M. [*in a low, solemn voice*]. Just now, before you came in, someone came to the door, and when I looked up I saw an angel standing there.

A YOUNG M. You were in a dream. Anybody can see an angel in his dreams.

WISE M. Oh, my God! It was not a dream! I was awake, waking as I am now. I tell you I was awake as I am now.

A YOUNG M. Some dream when they are awake, but they are the crazy, and who would believe what they say? Forgive me, Master, but that is what you taught me to say. That is what you said to the monk when he spoke of the visions of the saints and the martyrs.

ANOTHER YOUNG M. You see how well we remember your teaching.

WISE M. Out, out from my sight! I want someone with belief. I must find that grain the Angel spoke of before I die. I tell you I must find it, and you answer me with arguments. Out with you, out of my sight! [*The* YOUNG MEN *laugh.*]

A YOUNG M. How well he plays at faith! He is like the monk when he had nothing more to say.

WISE M. Out, out, this is no time for laughter! Out with you, though you are a king's son! [*They begin to hurry out.*]

A YOUNG M. Come, come; he wants us to find someone who will dispute with him.

> [*All go out.*]

WISE M. [*alone; he goes to the door at the side*]. I will call my wife. She will believe; women always believe. [*He opens the door and calls.*] Bridget! Bridget! [Bridget *comes in, wearing her apron, her sleeves turned up from her floury arms.*] Bridget, tell me the truth; do not say what you think will please me. Do you sometimes say your prayers?

Bridget. Prayers! No, you taught me to leave them off long ago. At first I was sorry, but I am glad now, for I am sleepy in the evening.

Wise M. But do you not believe in God?

Bridget. Oh, a good wife only believes what her husband tells her!

Wise M. But sometimes, when you are alone, when I am in the school and the children asleep, do you not think about the saints, about the things you used to believe in? What do you think of when you are alone?

Bridget [*considering*]. I think about nothing. Sometimes I wonder if the linen is bleaching white, or I go out to see if the cows are picking up the chickens' food.

Wise M. Oh, what can I do! Is there nobody who believes he can never die? I must go and find somebody! [*He goes towards the door, but stops with his eyes fixed on the hour-glass.*] I cannot go out; I cannot leave that; go and call my pupils again—I will make them understand—I will say to them that only amid spiritual terror, or only when all that laid hold on life is shaken can we see truth—but no, do not call them, they would answer as I have bid.

Bridget. You want somebody to get up an argument with.

Wise M. Oh, look out of the door and tell me if there is anybody there in the street! I cannot leave this glass; somebody might shake it! Then the sand would fall more quickly.

Bridget. I don't understand what you are saying. [*Looks out.*] There is a great crowd of people talking to your pupils.

Wise M. Oh, run out, Bridget, and see if they have found somebody that all the time while I was teaching understood nothing or did not listen.

Bridget [*wiping her arms in her apron and pulling down her sleeves*]. It's a hard thing to be married to a man of learning that must be always having arguments. [*Goes out and shouts through the kitchen door.*] Don't be meddling with the bread, children, while I'm out.

Wise M. [*kneels down*]. "*Confiteor Deo omnipotente beatæ Mariæ....*" I have forgotten it all. It is thirty years since I have said a prayer. I must pray in the common tongue, like a clown begging in the market, like Teigue the Fool! [*He prays.*] Help me, Father, Son, and Spirit!

> [B<small>RIDGET</small> *enters, followed by the* F<small>OOL</small>, *who is holding out his hat to her.*]

F<small>OOL</small>. Give me something; give me a penny to buy bacon in the shops, and nuts in the market, and strong drink for the time when the sun is weak.

B<small>RIDGET</small>. I have no pennies. [*To the* W<small>ISE</small> M<small>AN</small>.] Your pupils cannot find anybody to argue with you. There is nobody in the whole country who has enough belief to fill a pipe with since you put down the monk. Can't you be quiet now and not always wanting to have arguments? It must be terrible to have a mind like that.

W<small>ISE</small> M. I am lost! I am lost!

B<small>RIDGET</small>. Leave me alone now; I have to make the bread for you and the children.

W<small>ISE</small> M. Out of this, woman, out of this, I say! [B<small>RIDGET</small> *goes through the kitchen door.*] Will nobody find a way to help me! But she spoke of my children. I had forgotten them. They will believe. It is only those who have reason that doubt; the young are full of faith. Bridget, Bridget, send my children to me.

B<small>RIDGET</small> [*inside*]. Your father wants you; run to him now.

> [*The two* C<small>HILDREN</small> *come in. They stand together a little way from the threshold of the kitchen door, looking timidly at their father.*]

W<small>ISE</small> M. Children, what do you believe? Is there a Heaven? Is there a Hell? Is there a Purgatory?

F<small>IRST</small> C<small>HILD</small>. We haven't forgotten, father.

T<small>HE</small> O<small>THER</small> C<small>HILD</small>. Oh, no, father. [*They both speak together, as if in school.*] There is nothing we cannot see; there is nothing we cannot touch.

F<small>IRST</small> C<small>HILD</small>. Foolish people used to think that there was, but you are very learned and you have taught us better.

W<small>ISE</small> M. You are just as bad as the others, just as bad as the others! Do not run away; come back to me. [*The* C<small>HILDREN</small> *begin to cry and run away.*] Why are you afraid? I will teach you better—no, I will never teach you again. Go to your mother! no, she will not be able to teach them.... Help them, O God!...

The grains are going very quickly. There is very little sand in the uppermost glass. Somebody will come for me in a moment; perhaps he is at the door now! All creatures that have reason doubt. O that the grass and the plants could speak! Somebody has said that they would wither if they doubted. O speak to me, O grass blades! O fingers of God's certainty, speak to me! You are millions and you will not speak. I dare not know the moment the messenger will come for me. I will cover the glass. [*He covers it and brings it to the desk. Sees the* Fool, *who is sitting by the door playing with some flowers which he has stuck in his hat. He has begun to blow a dandelion head.*] What are you doing?

Fool. Wait a moment. [*He blows.*] Four, five, six.

Wise M. What are you doing that for?

Fool. I am blowing at the dandelion to find out what time it is.

Wise M. You have heard everything! That is why you want to find out what hour it is! You are waiting to see them coming through the door to carry me away. [Fool *goes on blowing.*] Out through the door with you! I will have no one here when they come. [*He seizes the* Fool *by the shoulders, and begins to force him out through the door, then suddenly changes his mind.*] No, I have something to ask you. [*He drags him back into the room.*] Is there a Heaven? Is there a Hell? Is there a Purgatory?

Fool. So you ask me now. When you were asking your pupils, I said to myself, if he would ask Teigue the Fool, Teigue could tell him all about it, for Teigue has learned all about it when he has been cutting the nets.

Wise M. Tell me; tell me!

Fool. I said, Teigue knows everything. Not even the cats or the hares that milk the cows have Teigue's wisdom. But Teigue will not speak; he says nothing.

Wise M. Tell me, tell me! For under the cover the grains are falling, and when they are all fallen I shall die; and my soul will be lost if I have not found somebody that believes! Speak, speak!

Fool [*looking wise*]. No, no, I won't tell you what is in my mind, and I won't tell you what is in my bag. You might steal away my thoughts. I met a bodach on the road yesterday, and he said, "Teigue, tell me how many pennies are in your bag; I will wager three pennies that there are not twenty pennies in your bag; let me put in my hand and count them." But I pulled the strings tighter, like this; and when I go to sleep every night I hide the bag where no one knows.

WISE M. [*goes towards the hour-glass as if to uncover it*]. No, no, I have not the courage. [*He kneels.*] Have pity upon me, Fool, and tell me!

FOOL. Ah! Now, that is different. I am not afraid of you now. But I must come nearer to you; somebody in there might hear what the Angel said.

WISE M. Oh, what did the Angel tell you?

FOOL. Once I was alone on the hills, and an angel came by and he said, "Teigue the Fool, do not forget the Three Fires; the Fire that punishes, the Fire that purifies, and the Fire wherein the soul rejoices for ever!"

WISE M. He believes! I am saved! The sand has run out.... [FOOL *helps him to his chair.*] I am going from the country of the seven wandering stars, and I am going to the country of the fixed stars!... I understand it all now. One sinks in on God; we do not see the truth; God sees the truth in us. Ring the bell. [FOOL *rings bell.*] Are they coming? Tell them, Fool, that when the life and the mind are broken the truth comes through them like peas through a broken peascod. Pray, Fool, that they may be given a sign and carry their souls alive out of the dying world. Your prayers are better than mine.

> [FOOL *bows his head.* WISE MAN's *head sinks on his arm on the books.* PUPILS *are heard singing as before, but now they come right into the room before they cease their song.*]

A YOUNG MAN. Look at the Fool turned bell-ringer!

ANOTHER. What have you called us in for, Teigue? What are you going to tell us?

ANOTHER. No wonder he has had dreams! See, he is fast asleep now. [*Goes over and touches him.*] Oh, he is dead!

FOOL. Do not stir! He asked for a sign that you might be saved. [*All are silent for a moment.*] ... Look what has come from his mouth ... a little winged thing ... a little shining thing.... It is gone to the door. [*The* ANGEL *appears in the doorway, stretches out her hands and closes them again.*] The Angel has taken it in her hands.... She will open her hands in the Garden of Paradise. [*They all kneel.*]

CURTAIN